JUDGE RANDALL

AND THE

TENURED PROFESSOR

JUDGE RANDALL
AND THE
TENURED PROFESSOR

TONY ROGERS

A Judge Randall Mystery

ISBN: 978-1-7356835-0-8 (Print)
ISBN: 978-1-7356835-1-5 (Ebook)

Published by Quinn Cove Books

Cover Design by Berge Design

To David, Veronica, and Sam

1

Judge Randall had been invited to give a talk at Harvard Divinity School on the topic, "Dispatches From The Real World, Justice As Seen By A Retired Judge." One of the panelists in the discussion to follow was Melvin Watson, an evangelical preacher who put his faith in God; another was Sara Vincent, a young MIT philosopher who put her faith in reason.

He had accepted the invitation because he knew and liked the dean of the school. Another reason was Judge Pat Knowles, his significant other and former colleague on the bench, who knew the talk would do Jim good, no matter how much he grumbled ahead of time.

The Divinity School was a few blocks across Kirkland Street in an area Jim called Fancy Land. By hedge fund standards, the houses were de minimis; by normal people standards, the houses were grand. A far cry from Jim's townhouse on a utilitarian side street, though not far in distance.

He walked with Pat to the Divinity School on the evening of the talk. It was summer and light lingered in the sky, a welcome relief from the cold, dark New England winter.

"You'll do fine," she said. Pat Knowles could not be called slender – she had proud shoulders and a solid body – yet her height made her look trim. Jim had known her for so long, first as a fellow judge and since both he and Pat had retired, his significant other, that her looks didn't register much of the time, yet as he was walking to what felt like his doom, he noticed how precise and beautiful the details of her face were.

Jim Randall carried himself with the authority he had shown in his years on the bench, his heavyset but not overweight body daring the ground to challenge his footsteps. When he wielded a gavel, he had been patient with witnesses, short-tempered with unprepared attorneys.

"Watson exists to provoke. He will be a complete ass," Jim said as he walked. "Professor Vincent I don't know, except by reputation."

"Which is?"

"Temperate. Measured. I expect she will separate Watson and me when we wrestle each other to the mat."

The Divinity School building is made of stone and built to last. It could be a bank headquarters or, in this gilded age, the second home of a hedge fund manager. It is near the Science Center and the Law School but across the river from the Business School.

"Why did I agree to do this?" Jim mouthed, as they neared the Divinity School, castle-like in the gathering dusk. Behind the school, construction trucks and cranes took a break until morning.

"You'll do fine."

He stopped walking. The evening air felt good going down. "The problem is, I don't know how to describe justice. I know it when I see it, but I don't know how to put it into words."

"Jim, we're going to be late. Come along."

He resumed walking. "Unsympathetic to my plight. There is no justice."

"Very funny," she said.

They entered the building with its echoing walls, and found the hall where Jim would speak. Folding chairs lined the floor and a table with three microphones stood on a raised podium. The room was slowly filling up.

The assistant dean approached, a woman in her forties named Fowler. Jim liked her the few times they had met. "Judge Randall, thank you. Our students are looking forward to this. And Judge Knowles, thank you for coming."

"Nice to see you again," Jim said.

"When we're ready, we'd like you to sit at the middle of the table, and Judge Knowles, we have reserved a front row seat for you."

Sara Vincent arrived then, brisk, trim and tailored, and Melvin Watson a few minutes later. Watson looked ready to go ten rounds; full cheeks, florid skin, flaring nostrils. The room had filled.

"Ready?" Dean Fowler asked.

"As I'll ever be," Jim said.

"Certainly," Sara Vincent said.

"Hell yeah," Melvin Watson said.

Jim, Watson, and Vincent took their seats on the podium. Dean Fowler, holding a microphone, began. "Thank you all for coming this evening. We have a special treat. Three important thinkers about justice are here tonight to share and contrast their views. Our main speaker is Judge Randall, with over twenty years experience as a trial judge on the Massachusetts Superior Court. During those years, Judge Randall presided over virtually every kind of civil and criminal case. Commenting on Judge Randall's remarks tonight will be Melvin Watson, minister of The Greater

Glory Evangelical Church, who has written extensively on justice, divine and otherwise, and Sara Vincent, the Paul S. and Tiffany E. Evans Professor of Ethics at MIT. Professor Vincent's latest book is *Philosophy: Blueprint to a Better Life or Parlor Game?* We will begin with a few remarks from Judge Randall. Judge Randall?"

Jim pulled his microphone closer to him and began. "Thank you, Dean Fowler. It is a pleasure to be here. Since I retired two years ago, I have ostensibly been writing a memoir with my former colleague on the bench, Patricia Knowles, but it turns out that I can't write except in legalese. Therefore I welcome this chance to spout off. The only danger I face is the lack of a gavel. In lieu of one, I throw myself on the mercy of the audience and of Melvin Watson, who as a man of God will no doubt be kind to me."

Jim looked to his left at Watson, who smiled. Jim noticed his ragged teeth; how did the man chew, side-to-side?

"Imperfect, is the way I would describe justice as seen from the bench. Not only are the judges, juries, lawyers, and litigants human, but statutes, case law, and precedent only cover some possible contingencies, leaving gaps in justice at the start of every trial. On a day-to-day level, I told myself to do the best I could and hope I was good enough, knowing on some days I wasn't. I will be interested to hear my fellow panelists on the view from the pulpit and the view from the classroom."

Jim spoke for another fifteen minutes, using several cases as examples of real-world choices that have to be made in court, showing how each choice could have affected the outcome, and asking the fundamental question in each case: Was justice served? Had there been a "right" choice just waiting to be made, or was the choice in each case a crapshoot?

That word gave Watson the opening he needed when his turn came. Although Jim's word was surrounded by dozens of other words, Watson pounced on it like a righteous man on a sinner. "God does not shoot craps. God the Almighty invented justice to save humans from their weakness and set them on a path of righteousness. Courts and classrooms that ignore His word are vehicles of perfidy." On and on in this vein; to call Watson's words inappropriate for an academic audience would be an understatement, but Jim had the view that Watson knew exactly what he was doing. Publicity in the name of God. God may not roll dice, but His servant Watson sure knew how to push buttons.

Sara Vincent didn't stand a chance. Her measured tone of voice, her unwillingness to accept unexamined thought, wilted in the roar of Watson's absolute certainty. "Many philosophers have accepted God," she explained. "In fact, the elimination of God from the equation is a fairly new phenomenon in philosophy. But it is fair to say that no philosopher has accepted God without rigorous questioning. Pascal, for example, after his own rigorous questioning, accepted God after deciding that a belief in God can't hurt and might help. Apparently rigorous questioning is what Reverend Watson fears since it can lead to non-doctrinaire answers like Pascal's."

Watson turned crimson. "I object! I fear nothing except God! And you, Professor, are making a personal attack!"

Jim intervened. "Objection overruled, Reverend. Darn, I wish I had my gavel."

Which made the audience laugh, which incensed Watson even more. Jim wasn't angry at Watson, he was amused. Surely Watson was vying for attention. Surely his minions were tweeting his provocations at this very moment.

What was God's attitude towards Twitter? #good? #bad? Jim must have smirked at the thought because Watson turned on him. "Are you scoffing at me, sir?"

"I am doing nothing of the sort, Reverend. I do not waste my scoffs. Your words are not worth a single scoff."

Watson stood and thundered. "I will not be mocked. Stand up, sir. Stand and face me."

"I choose not to."

"I shudder to think of your kind of 'justice'! Crassness. *You* judging people?" Watson reached for Jim's shirt collar. "Stand up!"

"Let go of me."

Watson wouldn't. He twisted and tugged Jim's shirt. "Stand up!"

Jim did and positioned his unflinching face inches from Watson's. "Let go of me."

Watson hesitated, stammered, then stomped off the podium. As he exited the auditorium he thundered, "Judgement Day is upon us! Only the righteous will be saved! Repent, ye sinners!"

The audience sat in stunned silence. No one knew what to do. Finally, Dean Fowler mounted the podium and turned to the audience. "Questions?"

Tittering. Shuffling of feet. A young man. "Judge Randall, will you press charges?"

"And play into the reverend's hands? No, thank you."

A young woman. "Professor Vincent, you made so much sense, but no one will remember what you said because the reverend turned to violence. Is that a metaphor?"

Sara Vincent smiled like someone who hated to let a smile escape. The tiniest opening of lips, like sipping through a straw. "I suppose so."

Jim clarified, "Don't mistake Reverend Watson for the norm. Even among the extreme wing of the evangelical church, he is extreme."

"Extremely loud!" someone in the audience shouted.

The audience had been looking for an excuse to laugh, and welcomed the chance now. After the laughter died, Dean Fowler adjourned the meeting.

"Which way are you walking?" Jim asked Sara Vincent.

"To the Square. I need a drink."

"Mind if Pat and I join you?"

They headed towards the Square. "Aren't you furious?" Vincent asked Jim.

"At Watson? No."

"But he attacked you."

"He grabbed my shirt, that's all. He was posturing. I didn't take it seriously."

"I was fuming."

"I couldn't tell. You don't show your emotions." Which was true, Vincent's face as they walked was absolutely expressionless. He was fascinated – Jim was a man who normally kept his emotions off his face, but compared to Sara Vincent's, his face was a billboard. Her face looked as if it were from the era before emotions were invented. Of course, it was dark now and the lights from Langdell Hall concealed faces. "I thought what you said – by the way –

was excellent. Watson plays on fear. Fear is his instrument, his language."

Sara Vincent seemed so interior it was painful to hear her speak. "I live in a bubble. I assume everyone is rational at some level."

"I used to. Then I became a judge."

They passed the Science Center and came to Harvard Yard. Jim was intrigued by Vincent. When he was intrigued by someone or something, Jim was tenacious.

They picked an underground restaurant in the Square that none of them had been to. The long bar was only half full.

They took a seat at the bar.

Sara Vincent's blonde hair was cropped severely short, the hair of an androgynous fashion model or of someone who pays no attention to her hair. Her fixed expression could be interpreted as boredom or contempt. Not an emotion to be seen on the surface. Jim likened her emotions to coal miners trapped by a cave-in. He was drawn to people like her because usually he could hear their emotions crying for rescue, but Vincent seemed an extreme case. "Your altercation with Watson is probably on YouTube by now," she said.

Vincent pulled out her phone, and sure enough, there was Watson fuming, standing, and grabbing, with Jim inches from his face. Vincent held it so Jim and Pat could see. "Were you going to hit him?"

"The thought never entered my mind. Bullies back down if you stand your ground, blows are rarely necessary, and at my age, inadvisable."

Vincent chewed her nails, Jim noticed when she tapped her screen again. Her nails were nubs. The Greater Glory website popped up on her phone. Already it had a glowing account of the evening. Reverend Watson literally standing up for God at Godless Harvard. Jim, looking old and cranky, and Sara Vincent sitting stonefaced, were lumped together as believers in reason who did not fear the awesome power of God. "God will show them no mercy on the Day of Reckoning!" thundered the webpage.

"Just what I thought," Jim said. "Watson orchestrated the whole fiasco ahead of time. This report was prepared hours, maybe days, ago."

Sara lived in the Aggasiz area past the Divinity School. Jim and Pat walked with her as far as the Science Center, then parted.

*

Melvin Watson's body was discovered in a sewer pipe behind the Divinity School the next morning. Large storm drains were being installed to control flooding during heavy rains, the Divinity School having been built atop a high water table. The operator of the crane that lifted the pipe had to be treated for shock when a body fell out.

Watson had been repeatedly hit in the head by a blunt instrument. The blows were heavy and many, the killing methodical.

"Talk about the altercation between the reverend and you," Jim was asked when he appeared at the police station to give a statement.

"It didn't amount to much. Watson was being his usual bombastic self and grabbed my shirt as an exclamation point of sorts. I think he planned the whole thing. You can watch it on YouTube."

"We already have," the detective said. "Had you met Reverend Watson before?"

"No. Nor Sara Vincent. Do you have any idea who did this?"

"Not yet. He has passionate followers and equally passionate haters."

Sara Vincent and Pat were waiting outside the interview room when Jim finished.

Pat looked up from the bench she was sitting on. "How did it go?"

"Apparently Watson has received plenty of death threats."

"What did they ask you?" Sara Vincent asked, worry in her voice.

"What I saw, what I heard, that sort of thing. Routine in this sort of case."

"Did they question you about Watson grabbing your shirt?"

"Of course. But since it is on YouTube, they had seen it for themselves."

"I don't know what they want from me."

"Relax, Sara. They just want to hear what happened, from your perspective. May I call you Sara, by the way?"

She nodded.

"You're nervous, aren't you?"

"I've never done this before."

"We'll wait for you."

When they were alone outside the interview room, Pat said to Jim, "Well, you've done it again. What it is about you and the grim reaper?"

Jim shrugged. "I wish I knew."

Sara Vincent lived six blocks from Jim, they discovered when she, Pat, and Jim left the police station together. She seemed rattled. "They made me feel as if I had done something wrong."

"The first couple of times I was questioned by the police, I felt the way you do."

"You've been questioned before?"

"It's sort of a hobby of mine."

Her head shook in a little spasm. "Why would they think I had anything to do with it?"

"I'm sure they don't. It just seemed that way to you."

Most of the houses in mid-Cambridge were converted into condos long ago. From the outside, the condos look modest, but the prices aren't – location, location, location, mid-Cambridge being between Harvard and MIT. Mid-Cambridge probably has more advanced degrees per square block than most big cities.

"Pat and I have been through this before. Prepare for a flurry of press interest. It will seem as if the attention will never end. Take heart, it will."

2

Fiery Preacher Found Dead Behind Harvard Divinity School
Evangelical Minister's Body Stuffed In Sewer Pipe
Who Killed The Avenging Preacher?

Many people wanted to, according to the news accounts that followed the murder. Until his death, Watson was little known outside the evangelical world. Years ago, he had established a small settlement of like-minded people in Maine – The Greater Glory – which had grown into the size of a small town. They did good works in surrounding communities but otherwise kept to themselves. After flourishing in the '90s, the settlement had fallen on hard times, partly because of competition from a commune that had split off from Watson's over doctrinal differences – The Greater Good. The local newspapers had run numerous stories about verbal spats between followers of The Greater Good and followers of The Greater Glory. Sometimes the local police had to be called to separate the followers before blows were struck.

"Nothing like a good fight among God's messengers," Jim commented to Pat when he finished reading.

Jim found himself wondering about Sara Vincent. The only time she betrayed any emotion was at the police station, where she had been noticeably nervous. On the panel, she had been logic personified, unruffled by Watson or the audience. Jim had the impression of a woman who lived in a world of one, dedicated to reason, no emotions or outsiders allowed.

Yet he liked her. Why? Because he saw in her an extreme version of himself? Because – let's face it – as hard as she tried to be plain, she was pretty, and Natalie, Jim's sister, said he had a weakness for beautiful women.

The FBI was investigating Watson's killing, and Jim ought to touch base with Enrique Montgomery, the young head of the Boston office. They had become close professionally during the aftermath of the Boston Marathon bombing. Enrique had plenty of street smarts but so far had resisted adopting the swagger and jargon of the FBI. Jim was old enough to remember J. Edgar Hoover, a scoundrel and a hypocrite if there ever were one. Enrique was a new breed of agent.

"Hi, Enrique. Jim Randall here."

"You're in the news again. And when you're in the news, murder shall follow. How are you?"

"Good. And you?"

"Hungry for a little excitement. Grateful you called. Yes, we've been asked to help in the Watson murder. I assume that's why you called."

"Yes. Anything?"

"Not so far. Only old rumors that Watson may have had an eye for young girls."

"What is it about the religious fringe? The more fervent the belief, the greater the sin."

"Something like that," Enrique said.

"Maybe that's why I don't believe. I'm sin-free."

Enrique laughed. "Any thoughts on Watson's murder?"

"None. I read a little about his commune in Maine this morning and am struck by the parallels with the militias I encountered after the Marathon bombings. But I don't know what to make of that."

"Be moderate in all things."

"Even more important given the human propensity to go to extremes. Let me know if you find anything, will you? I have a personal stake in this given that Melvin Watson challenged me in front of an audience."

"Made you mad enough to kill, did it?"

"You're joking, aren't you?"

"Of course I am. You're a curmudgeon but not a killer. How about Sara Vincent, could she be involved?"

"I very much doubt it. I've only known her for twenty-four hours, but she seems an unlikely killer, to put it mildly. If she had murderous thoughts, she would process them internally and get as much satisfaction as if she had pulled the trigger."

"An academic, you're saying."

"An extreme example."

Ever since Jim's first post-retirement involvement with the law, he had grown more inclined to trust his gut. That ran counter to all his legal training and his self-discipline on the bench. It was as if he had gone from one extreme to the other. Well, that was not entirely true; an exaggeration; more a case of the needle being nudged from one side of the center to the other, but it seemed to him an extreme change because he was so even-keeled for so long.

And his instinct told him to start investigating the Watson murder in academia, even though he didn't think that Sara Vincent was the killer. He didn't know why his instinct pointed in that direction – maybe because the panel had been held at the Divinity School and Sara Vincent taught at MIT. If he were still on the bench he would immediately dismiss such an instinct, but free of his robe and his gavel, he could indulge his instincts. MIT had an excellent philosophy department, and wouldn't it be delicious if Watson's murder were the result of a blood feud between reason and religion?

First stop, the dean of Harvard Divinity School, George Barrows. Jim had known Barrows casually for years. They had met in Vermont, where Barrows rented a house for his family every summer. Barrows came by the deanship by way of construction, having joined his father's construction company fresh out of college with an eye to someday running it. When it became clear that George needed more education to be a successful businessman, he went to business school at night, and when it became clear to George that business, family or no, was not for him, he turned to the study of religion, getting a degree in ancient religions and eventually being named dean. A jovial man in his late fifties, he looked more like a carnival barker than a divinity school dean, but was an excellent fundraiser and liked by all.

Barrows had a jolly body, but underneath the years of pleasure one could discern the muscles he had used for digging ditches. "Jim. Good to see you alive and well. Goddamn, that's the last time I'll invite you to speak! How are you?"

"Fine, George. You going to rent the usual place this summer?"

"Unsure. My youngest will be working in Israel this summer, and Marge and I may want to do something different. Vermont wouldn't be the same without the kids."

"You and Marge will still enjoy yourselves, George. And Pat and I could come down and join you for a dinner or two, as usual."

"I'd like that, Jim. We're not getting younger. Enjoy it while you can. What can I do for you?"

"Trace your thought patterns leading up to the event the other night. Who suggested Watson for the panel?"

"Sara Vincent," the dean said.

"I thought so. How did she know him?"

"Claimed she didn't but thought The Greater Glory would present a useful contrast to the rational approach to life of the law and academia."

"She's right, although given how the evening ended, probably not a good idea."

"I personally knew little about Watson before Sara's suggestion. I knew a group of followers had split from him and formed their own group, but that's about all I know. We have a professor who studies fringe groups who might be able to give you more information. His name is Pierre Reynolds. Want to meet him?"

*

Pierre Reynolds turned out to be a young African-American who wore a bow tie and a neatly tailored suit. A man who spent time in clothing stores. "Dean Barrows said you are interested in fringe groups."

"One group in particular, The Greater Glory."

"And you are interested because of Watson's murder?"

"Correct."

Reynolds shook his head. "Horrible, horrible. To think his body was found behind the school. I shudder."

"Tell me about the rivalry between his group and the splinter group."

"Ah, Greater Glory v. Greater Good! Now you're talking. Hatred, pure hatred. Glen Masters, the founder of The Greater Good, split from Watson because Watson's group had become devoted to the glory of Melvin Watson, not God. Masters considered Watson a charlatan."

Reynolds rose from his desk. He was a small man who moved with precision. He seemed to be sure of himself but not sure how others would take him; wariness cloaked in precision.

"I am telling you, Judge, that there is no better soap opera than what goes on inside a religious commune. Duplicity, envy, venality, sex, you name it. I am waiting with bated breath for the reality show about true believers; no one would believe it."

"Was Masters's splinter group Watson's mortal enemy?"

"You mean, would Glen Masters or one of his followers murder Melvin Watson?"

"Yes."

"The answer is no, an emphatic no. In my opinion, Melvin Watson was the one capable of violence. Masters is a peaceable man except about Watson. Masters fervently believes that Watson betrayed the rationale and purpose of The Greater Glory, yet like many cult followers, he couldn't bring himself to break entirely with the cult and only moved to the adjoining property. The Two Greaters, as I call them, share a border. Very symbolic. I've seen it with cults in general. They attract believers by claiming it's the group against the world, then start bickering among themselves until it becomes one faction against the other. Sometimes the fighting becomes so fierce that one or more factions splinter from the original cult, and those disputes are the most vicious of all. I don't know what's going to happen without Watson. Both groups will probably fail. Heathens versus the faithful is not enough for true believers, they need the conflict to be personalized, e.g., Watson v. Masters."

"Tell me about life within the groups."

Reynolds picked up his pace. He paced with his hands behind his back, his trim frame leaning forward, a sailboat tacking into the wind. "How long do you have? Fascinating subject, life within a cult. Weird practices, the abandonment of individual will, slavish devotion to a leader who doesn't directly claim to be the descendent of God but strongly implies it. I can't give you an authoritative account of what went on in The Greater Glory under Melvin Watson, or in The Greater Good under Glen Masters. They guard their practices and habits jealously from the outside world – the CIA could take lessons – but Watson liked young women, very young women, in multiples. The thing that interests me about that phenomenon, which isn't uncommon in cults, is why the older women in the cult put up with it. Their daughters were the ones Watson used and spit out."

"How about Masters's group?"

"Again, not certain, but I think Masters's group went the other direction, sex only for the purpose of procreation.

Members of The Greater Good dressed like penitents, sackcloth and ashes."

Reynolds stopped pacing. He stood thinking. "Your next question is, who do I think killed Melvin Watson? I have not the slightest idea. Cults come and go, very few leaders get assassinated. But you might want to talk to Masters. It's possible a member of The Greater Good carried his hatred of Watson to an extreme, with or without Masters's knowledge."

*

The Greater Good – Glen Masters's commune – consisted of a cluster of rickety houses hidden in the woods beside a small lake near the New Hampshire border. There was no identifying sign. If Pierre Reynolds had not given Jim directions, he would have whizzed right by the dirt road that served as a driveway. A barking dog greeted him.

Jim got out of his car. A young man approached. Not friendly. "What do you want?"

"To see Glen Masters."

The young man turned with seeming impatience and walked towards one of several houses clustered around a clearing. The houses had the look of impermanence, like movie Western storefronts that could be blown away in a stiff wind.

A moment later, a tall man walked out of a house, tall enough to have to lean over to get through the door without hitting his head. He looked to be about fifty, although his face was so lined it was hard to tell. He pushed thick hair out of his eyes as he approached Jim.

"You wanted to see me?" His voice was glue.

Jim extended his hand. "Jim Randall."

Masters squinted at Jim. "Who are you? Why are you here?"

"A retired judge. I was with Melvin Watson the night he died."

Masters ceased movement, as if a pause button had been pushed. He came to life and shook Jim's hand.

"Let's go inside." Masters gestured to the house. On the way, he spoke to the young man, who stood a respectful distance away. "It's fine, Saul. Go about your business."

Masters opened the door. The inside of the house belied the exterior. Nothing flimsy about it. What Jim saw as he walked through the door was a leather sofa and flat screen TV, and at the other end of the room, a large table, computer, ledgers, lined paper.

"Have a seat." Masters gestured to the sofa. A dull-eyed woman appeared from the back. "We have a visitor," Masters told her. To Jim he said, "My wife, Rachel."

"Pleased to meet you, Mrs. Masters. I'm Jim Randall."

"Can I get you anything? Coffee, tea?" Rachel Masters had a beleaguered look. Earlier in her life, her eyes must have been bright, now they were anything but.

"No, thanks."

She left the room as unobtrusively as she entered, and Masters began. "You were a judge?"

"Yes, Massachusetts Superior Court. The trial court. I retired two years ago."

"Is your visit here unofficial?"

"Very. I was on the panel with Melvin Watson on the night he died."

Masters nodded. "I saw him grab you on YouTube."

"I take it you have not exiled yourself from technology."

Masters's eyes brightened. "We choose to live removed from society but we haven't renounced its conveniences."

"Has Watson's group?"

"Hard to know what they're doing now. I haven't been let back in since I left. Before I left, they had."

"Cut themselves off from the world?"

"Yes."

"I'm confused. I was told that you and your group live like penitents."

"We're against sin, not technology. Watson's group, on the other hand, shunned the outside world but debauched like crazy inside theirs."

"Is that why you split off from his group?"

"We have a daughter, Judge Randall. She's a teenager now, but she was only ten at the time. It wasn't safe for her. Do you understand?"

"So Watson's reputation for liking young girls was accurate?"

"Absolutely."

"Why didn't you report this to the police?"

"I did, but it accomplished nothing. Fortunately, God's vengeance is mightier than your justice. Look what happened to Watson."

"He was hit over the head with a blunt instrument. Did God do that?"

"You know what I mean."

"If Watson lived as you say he did, sounds like anyone with a young daughter had motive to kill him."

"If you're suggesting I did it, you're wrong. By taking half his group with me when I founded The Greater Good, I punished him in the most painful possible way. Imagine what losing half his flock did to a man with a God-size ego."

"Are you pleased he's dead?"

"To an extent, I won't deny that. But in a strange sort of way, I miss him. He served a useful purpose."

Jim nodded. "Everyone needs an enemy."

"I have no idea who killed Melvin Watson. If you line up all the people who wanted to, the line would stretch from here to Boston, maybe to Philadelphia. He delighted in pissing people off, but as to who killed him, I haven't a clue."

Jim's mind idled on his drive home. Whereas Watson had seemed like an actor who has mastered the lines but doesn't believe them, Masters seemed – relatively speaking – sincere, bitter but sincere. Jim was inclined to believe he didn't kill Watson, but there was something "off" about a group that lived in the woods within shouting distance of a group it hated.

He wanted to tell Pat his impressions of Glen Masters. He pulled to the side of the road and called her.

"Not a screw loose, like Watson, but strange."

"Do you think he did it?" It was good to hear her voice.

"No, but maybe one of his followers."

"Are you coming straight here or stopping in Cambridge first?"

"Straight into your loving arms."

"Sing it."

He sang a bar or two.

Quickly, "On second thought, don't."

3

Sara Vincent had never been in The Long Gone, a coffeehouse that since Jim's retirement had become his hangout of choice. "Funky," was her pronouncement when she met Jim there.

"Please don't tell me it's very Brooklyn. I hate Brooklyn."

Her expression didn't change. "No, I won't. Why did you ask to meet me?"

"I visited Glen Masters's group, The Greater Good."

That elicited a flicker. "Really? Why?"

"You have to ask?" He filled her in on what he found. The baristas of The Long Gone were in fine voice behind them."Harriet! Cinnamon mocha latte! Richard, double espresso!"

"So, what do you think?" Jim asked.

"It scares me."

"Wait, do you mean The Greater Good or The Long Gone?"

"The Long Gone. Too funky for me."

Her hair and expression were tight for a reason, Jim mused.

"What did you think of Glen Masters?" She asked with what Jim took as timidity. Why had her voice suddenly lost resolve?

"He seemed normal compared to Watson. I don't think he is our killer."

"Me neither."

"Oh? Do you know him?"

"I've met him."

"Really? No kidding."

"My family vacationed near his compound when I was a child. I got to know him a little."

"That explains a lot of things, like why you suggested Melvin Watson be on the panel with us."

"Glen and I are occasionally in touch. I know about his commune and his dispute with Watson."

"I'm wrapping my mind around this. You strike me as the polar opposite of Glen Masters. It never occurred to me that you know him."

She nodded. "If our families hadn't vacationed near each other, Glen and I would never have met."

"Why didn't you tell me this before?"

"I didn't think it mattered."

"Even after Watson died?"

"What difference would my knowing Glen Masters have made?"

"You and I were on a panel with Melvin Watson, the now *deceased* Melvin Watson, Glen Masters's mortal enemy. That's the difference it would have made."

She shrugged. "I have a class to teach. I have to get back."

"I'll walk with you, I love East Cambridge." He had much more to ask her about Masters, but he wanted to know her better. He waited until he could see the live poultry shop, one of Jim's touchstones – Jim needed touchstones. "You mind my asking, are you married?"

"No."

"Divorced?"

"Never married. Why?"

"Just to know you a little better." He noticed she seemed looser as she walked than sitting in The Long Gone. "I'll bet you're a skier or a hiker."

That elicited a noticeable change of expression. Success! "How did you know?"

"You move like an athlete."

"I ran track in college. And I'll be late to class if I don't hurry."

Beauty Show Row, another of Jim's touchstones, was up ahead. "Want me to call a cab?"

"No, but I'll make better time by myself. I'll say goodbye here."

She was already on the move, at twice his pace. She waved over her shoulder as she departed.

He let her get far enough ahead so she wouldn't feel stalked, then continued in the direction of Boston and Beacon Hill, where Pat lived. They spent most nights together but kept separate homes. Tonight he needed a Pat fix. He let himself in with his key and found her at the kitchen table, writing. Just as he entered, she flung her hands above her head in a triumphant V. "Done!"

"What?" he deadpanned.

"Our memoir. *My* memoir! Finished!"

"Finally."

"Sarcasm? From the man who has been working on one chapter for two years?"

"I haven't been steadily working. I could've gone much faster if I had wanted to. Anyway, this calls for champagne."

"I don't have any."

"I'll settle for red wine." He kissed her. "Congratulations. Scribe."

"You are pushing your luck, buddy."

He smiled. "May I read it?"

"If you promise to feel guiltier and guiltier with every page."

"I promise."

Pat's memoir was about her years as a trial judge. He had read bits and pieces of it before but that night read the whole thing and was overwhelmed. It was so human, so poignant. No one would believe the stern judge they had seen on the bench could write such a warm and personal book.

He finished at 3 a.m. Pat had been asleep for hours. He tried to sleep but couldn't.

He was drinking coffee in the kitchen when she got up. "Morning," she yawned. "I read your memoir."

"The whole thing?"

"I skimmed the parts I had read before, but yes, the whole thing. I couldn't put it down. It deserves wide readership and rousing cheers. What a wonderful job. Congratulations."

She sat down beside him. "Really?"

"You don't believe me?"

"Oh, I believe you mean it, I just can't believe I may have written something good. I was flying blind."

"I especially love the last chapter, where you merge the professional and the personal so seamlessly. Beautiful."

"Stop. Too much praise," she said. "I prefer, not bad, could be better. Say that."

"No. Hold me in contempt, I don't care. You have written an important document, one that will be read by law students and lay people alike."

She stood and poured herself coffee. "Don't expect me to lighten up on you just because you praise me."

"Never would I think that."

"Because I'm going to be as tough on you as usual when you deserve it."

"I expect no less."

"I mean it."

"You need to learn to accept compliments better."

She turned, coffee cup in hand. "Maybe if you compliment me more I would."

"Sara Vincent knew Glen Masters from when she was a teen. Their families summered near each other."

"And?"

"And she clammed up when I pushed her on what she knew about him."

Pat came to the table and sat down. "What do you think it means?"

"She's a very private person, so it may not mean anything. For example, she shut down when I asked her if she was married."

"Is she?"

"Never has been. But I don't know what her reticence about Masters means, if anything."

"But you intend to find out."

"If I can find time in my busy writing schedule. Seriously, Pat, congratulations."

*

Jim wanted to know more about Sara Vincent. When Jim googled her, he found that she had five books to her credit. Academic honors as a teacher and a student. Not a single shred of personality revealed online. Not a tweet, not a photo, not a Facebook page. Her work was her personality.

Unraveling Sara became a more pressing challenge than finding Melvin Watson's killer, at least while Jim was thinking about her. When he stopped thinking about her, Watson in a drain pipe returned to the number one position. What really interested him about Watson's death was the dueling fundamentalists angle; it had the All-American ingredients – competition, religion, and violence. He hoped – he prayed – that a God-fearing fundamentalist killed the fiery preacher, not some namby-pamby atheist.

Unravel your thoughts, Jim. You hate hypocrisy, that is a given, but the additional impetus to finding Watson's killer was how orchestrated Watson's performance had been the night of the panel. He had manufactured his umbrage – nothing Jim said or did had warranted it. He had it up his sleeve like a magician's scarf, ready to unfurl at the optimal moment. Had Watson miscalculated? Had his show of umbrage somehow backfired and led to his murder? Did he have an accomplice primed to rough up an enemy outside the Divinity School and somehow Watson – not the intended target – ended up in a drain pipe? If so, who had been the original target? Not Jim, he had never met Watson. Maybe Sara, who knew Watson's rival. And if so, who was the accomplice? A far-fetched theory, Jim admitted, but better than a blank slate.

One of the things he enjoyed about his newfound second career as an amateur sleuth was its freedom of thought; he could start with a cockamamie theory and wind his circuitous way to the truth without the pressure of ruling on motions and weighing evidence on the record. Being a judge was to adhere to sheet music, being an amateur sleuth was to be a jazz musician.

He went to bed much later than Pat that night and mumbled something under his breath as he climbed under the covers.

"What did you say?" Pat asked from her side of the bed.

"I thought you were asleep."

"I was. What did you say? It sounded like 'hellfire and damnation.'"

"Go back to sleep."

*

One thing he liked about Sara Vincent was he didn't have to waste words. She didn't, so he needn't.

"Coffee?"

The Long Gone at noon. Croissants and bagels, but no sandwiches. Thank God no sandwiches! He didn't understand sandwiches. Why put meat between bread? Joyce, his late wife, had little use for whimsy, and had explained – none too patiently – that sandwiches allowed a person to eat with his or her hands. To which Jim replied, I hate eating with my hands. (He was not a man to give up easily, especially when he was out of step with the zeitgeist – zeitgeist was another thing he didn't understand.)

Sara seemed intimidated by the hissing of hot milk and the baristas' cries. "Everything okay?" he asked.

"Why?"

"Sara, is it a crime to like you? You seem intimidated, I notice."

She shifted her weight, ending up with her left elbow on the table. "You were right, the press has been hounding me. I've been ducking as best I could."

"You did well. I only saw you mentioned once or twice."

"But my picture! Did you see my picture?"

"I thought it was very nice. Didn't you?"

"I don't want people to recognize me!"

"Relax, this too shall pass. You will be like used Kleenex in a week or two. I want to learn more about Glen Masters. Think back to when you met him and tell me everything you remember."

Sara withdrew her elbow from the table and sat up straight. Jim watched her eyes as she remembered. They flickered with a moment of recognition. Just once. So that was how her face revealed emotion. He liked that; it was so out of step with the norm of an outgoing country. Good for her!

"I must have been eight at the time. He seemed ancient, although he was only in his thirties. My mother especially liked him, but Dad did too. Glen had dinner at our house several times. By the time I entered junior high – I know this sounds strange coming from me – he had come to seem dashing, I guess because he was handsome and sure of himself. I didn't know many boys in high school, but the ones I knew all were tongue-tied and awkward around girls."

"Did he ever make a pass at you?"

"No."

"Is that a flat no, or a nuanced no?"

"He never made a pass at me."

For a moment, she seemed nonplussed. He waited, then said, "But?"

"He never made a pass at me. Never. Melvin Watson did, but not Glen."

"Stop there. Back up. Melvin Watson made a pass at you? When?"

"Glen took me with him to Watson's compound once when I was thirteen, said he wanted me to see the compound for myself. And when we got there, Watson's wife distracted Glen for enough time for Watson to hit on me."

Sara's expression didn't change while she told this, but Jim felt a chill. "That must have been upsetting."

"Very. I never went back, and Glen never suggested it. He could tell I was rattled and asked if I was okay, and I said yes. 'Good,' he said. He had wanted me to see for himself. It was just before he broke with Watson, and I think he was hoping to use young, impressionable me to influence my parents to support him in his feud."

"Did they?"

"Mom did, to the extent Dad would let her. She was an empty vessel in search of something to fill her up. Dad was too hard-headed to support a fringe group, even though he liked Glen."

"Your parents must have been appalled to hear that Watson hit on you."

"Keep in mind that Watson didn't lay a hand on me. It was subtler than that."

"Still, your parents must have been appalled."

"They didn't know until later when Glen told them. He told them to bolster his case against Watson."

"Watson sounds sick to me."

"My mother was a lost soul. She loved me but had not the slightest idea what was best for me, and Dad was too unsure of himself outside the realm of business to know what to do with me. I learned to fend for myself."

"Were you the only child?"

"No."

"Brother? Sister?"

"Brother."

Jim waited in vain for her to say more. When she didn't, he said, "Have I touched a nerve?"

No flicker of recognition. "My brother committed suicide when I was sixteen. He killed himself on the property line between The Greater Glory and The Greater Good. He stood at the gate between the compounds and cut his throat. We never found out why. He didn't leave a note."

"This is terrible, Sara. My heart breaks."

She shook her head. "I got over it a long time ago. We as a family never summered there again."

Jim listened to the espresso machine releasing its steam. "Thank you for telling me this. It must have been hard for you."

"I haven't talked about it for years and years."

"Then I'm especially grateful."

She had one more thing to add. "Watson was a sexual predator, but as far as I know, he only liked girls. But he tolerated the sexual practices of his followers, whatever they were. I can only assume my brother was subjected to sexual harassment by one of his followers."

"You don't have to say more. I'm so sorry."

4

Jim's second home was perched on a ridge overlooking the Connecticut River, north of Brattleboro, Vermont. In the right slant of light, the Connecticut River formed a shifting, silvery border between Vermont and New Hampshire. Light was Jim's religion. Light and luck – there you had it, philosophy, religion, and nature, all rolled into two.

On the drive up, he said to Pat, "The Greater Glory sounds like a summer camp for deviants. Hallelujah and praise the Lord."

"Sara's brother being one victim."

"Correct. It's becoming clear why Sara closed down, although maybe she had a reclusive personality to begin with."

Pat said, "She's introverted by nature and her childhood experiences pushed her over the edge. That's my guess."

"Mine, too."

"What do you think will become of The Greater Glory now that its leader is dead?"

"Probably disband."

"But only after internecine warfare is my guess. When you think God talks to you, you don't give up easily."

"Warfare between the two Greaters. Beautiful."

"What do you make of Masters after what Sara told you about him?"

"I still think he is cut from a different cloth than Watson." Sometimes it was hard for Jim to tell if Pat was speaking or he was, that was how closely their thoughts could track.

But there would be times when their thoughts seemed jarringly at odds, and he couldn't predict when those times would be, which was disconcerting. He liked being close to her – he had never experienced such closeness before – but it carried risks.

"This is your first time up here since you finished the memoir. Do you miss the writing?" he asked.

"Yes."

"Any thoughts what you'll do to fill the gap?"

"No. For the moment, I welcome a respite."

Pat paused, "Are Sara's parents alive?"

"I don't know."

"You haven't asked?"

"Not that question. She doesn't invite small talk."

"Nor do you offer it."

They arrived at the house under a half moon. The ridge behind the house was outlined as if in pencil. From the living room window, the Connecticut River valley looked more three dimensional than usual, its highlands more visible, its depths more hidden. Light, again.

He slept like a baby.

He awoke with a fresh slant on things.

He hadn't spent much time on the MIT campus. It was high time. When he got home from Vermont, he took the Red Line to Kendall Square and walked MIT's vast industrial-looking campus. He didn't know what he was looking for – Watson had not been killed there; Harvard had that honor – but his investigative method was to absorb the atmosphere of the site or sites that might lead to a solution. "Investigative method"! Listen to yourself,

Randall, you pompous ass, you have been an amateur sleuth for too short a time to settle on a "method."

The MIT campus has green spaces and lots of public art and some striking contemporary architecture, but one can quickly tell it is the home of a school that makes or discovers things, as opposed to discussing things. A no bullshit place. He preferred that, although he did not speak math. He walked the campus wondering if a place like MIT attracted zipped-tight people like Sara Vincent, or did the campus zip them tight? What would it be like to be a philosopher at a no bullshit school? Engineering depended on precise measurements, philosophy thrived on analogy. Logic was a crude instrument compared to math.

Yet he, Judge Randall, formerly of the Massachusetts Superior Court, was drawn to logic more than to numbers. He suspected Sara Vincent was, too. He continued walking until he came to a sleek glass building that housed the Media Lab and thought of the adage, "people who live in glass houses." Consider, for a moment, Sara Vincent's personality enclosed by glass walls, not steel or brick. What if something shattered the walls, like a brother's suicide. Would it let her out or shut her down?

He came to the Red Line and realized he had unintentionally walked in a circle. Depressed that he had made little progress, he took the T back to Harvard Square, back to the familiar, bullshit and all.

A text from Enrique Montgomery, the head agent of the Boston office of the FBI, reached Jim as he surfaced at the Out-of-Town newsstand. Enrique was relatively new to the Boston office, but Jim was impressed with him.

"Drop by my office and I'll bring you up to date."

So he returned to the Red Line, getting off this time at Park Street and walking to Government Center. He could transfer to the Green Line and save himself a walk, but he hated to change lines.

Enrique's spartan office, a familiar place by now. Pictures of his children on his desk. Handsome kids, beaming kids.

"Here's what we've learned," Enrique said. He looked especially young today, maybe because of his baby blue shirt. Dark eyes too serious by half but hiding a grin. "Glen Masters and Melvin Watson filed numerous charges against each other over the years, but the cases were either dropped or thrown out of court. All except one: a charge of kidnapping against Watson and The Greater Glory that resulted in prison time for one of his followers. Was the follower a true believer who would do anything for his spiritual leader, or was the follower blackmailed into taking the fall? No one knows."

Jim nodded. "Watson allowed his followers to indulge their most debauched desires, then cleansed their sins with talk of God. Loyalty was sure to follow. Have you questioned Masters about Watson's murder?"

"The Maine police did and learned nothing that sheds light. Masters has an airtight alibi. In the hospital for arrhythmia the night of the murder. We are running checks on all known followers of Watson and Masters. Kooks running loose, but so far no killer."

"Where did the money come from to fund The Greater Glory?"

"Much of it from Richie Monroe, the techie who developed the popular app, Quacking Ducks. After Monroe sold the app to Apple for $20 million, he became disgusted at how easily he had become wealthy and threw lots of money Watson's way. He also raised money for Watson through crowdsourcing. Watson had more than he needed to keep The Greater Glory afloat."

"What would a young guy like Monroe see in a group like The Greater Glory?"

"Sex, God, and crowdsourcing. Nerd heaven."

"Apparently Watson thought of everything," Jim said.

"Not everything or he'd still be alive. By the way, the police found the murder weapon. A length of pipe used by the construction crew, buried in a ditch behind the Divinity School. It wouldn't have been found except that rain had washed most of the dirt away. No fingerprints but a trace of blood matched Watson's DNA."

Jim walked home when he was done with Enrique. Walking was his therapy, his meditation. He was unaware of his surroundings until he came to the Cambridge side of the Longfellow Bridge and MIT's Sloan School of Management. Across the Charles River, the Boston skyline tried to look imposing, when in fact it did a good job of looking human and should leave it at that. He took the sidewalk beside the river (and the damn Memorial Drive with its ceaseless speeders), and gazed at the sawtooth skyline.

What would compel someone to kill an evangelical preacher? Doctrinal differences? Personal hatred? Sexual jealousy? Money? Family? All of the above? None of the above?

The river looked scalloped, the sky mottled. Why can't humans behave humanely? Who are we to preach to others when we screw up so often?

He thought back to when he first moved to Cambridge. The river was much cleaner now, but Boston was as parochial as ever. More multicultural to be sure, but as constricted as ever. Boundaries are not drawn by cartographers, they are defined by psychologists.

He walked until he came to the Massachusetts Avenue bridge and hopped the bus to Harvard Square, getting off before the last stop and circumnavigating the Central Library. Cambridge was an okay place to live.

Pat greeted him at the door. Her expression asked the inevitable question. "Well?"

"Don't pressure me," he said. "This isn't easy."

At Duck, Duck, Goose that evening, Pat asked why he was in a funk. He replied that if one wasn't in a funk half of the time, one was dodging reality.

"Have you run into a roadblock?"

"The way forward is always murky at this stage."

"Take your mind off murder. Do something you like."

"I like having dinner with you at our favorite restaurant."

"There you go. Feeling better now?"

"Couldn't be happier."

"See how easy it was?"

He raised his glass to her. "Cheers."

"This tastes good," she said.

"A Cahors from southwest France. The grape is malbec."

"I thought malbec was Argentinian."

"By way of France."

"Live and learn."

"It's time I paid Ted a visit."

Ted Conover, assistant district attorney, frequent presence in Jim's courtroom, and longtime friend. His office near the courthouse was all work.

"I wondered when I'd hear from you." Ted had the look of the perpetually overworked, the personality of the unfazed.

"When I was good and ready."

"We don't have a suspect yet."

"I assumed not."

"But you have undoubtedly solved the crime."

"Absolutely. But I'm not going to tell you who did it."

Ted pursed his lips. "Good. Maintain suspense."

"Seriously, any leads besides the lead pipe?"

Ted pulled his chair closer to his desk. "The FBI is taking the lead in the investigation. They are treating it as a hate crime until proven otherwise. The dean of the Divinity School, faculty members, tradespeople working the construction project have all been questioned. No one saw Watson being attacked."

"Did the attack happen where the body was found?"

"We think so. There are no signs that the body was moved."

"Couldn't the rain have washed away signs it was moved?"

"Believe it or not, we and the FBI thought of that."

"Sorry, Ted, I shouldn't be telling you how to do your job."

Ted smiled. "But that's not going to stop you."

"I'm assuming Sara Vincent has been questioned."

"She has."

"Did you learn anything?"

"She professes not to know anything about the murder. She has referenced Watson's group, The Greater Glory, in her course on religion and philosophy, which is why she suggested him for the panel. Otherwise, she could shed no light. By the way, what did you do that night after the panel?"

"Are you serious?"

Ted shrugged. "I questioned Sara Vincent, I have to question you."

Jim stared. "Pat and I had a drink with Sara, escorted her partway home, then said goodnight."

"Did you leave together?"

"As opposed to one at a time? Of course we left together."

"Sometimes Pat stays at her place on Beacon Hill, according to you."

"Yes, sometimes she does. But the night of the panel she stayed with me. At my townhouse in Cambridge, Massachusetts, in the US of A, if you're not sure I'm telling the truth."

Ted smiled. "We've already talked to her. She confirmed your story. Course she could be lying."

"Cut it out, Ted. We've known each other a long time."

"Easy, Jim. I was joking. I believe you. But you have to admit you had motive."

"Because Watson made a fool of himself? How is that motive for murder?"

"You know what I mean. Oh, never mind. Let's drop the subject."

Coffee at The Long Gone to calm down. Relax, Jim, he was just doing his job. You know he believes you. But you do get yourself in these ridiculous situations.

So? Pugnacious Jim answered.

His phone beeped. A text from Ted. "Sorry, Jim. You have to admit, you'd be the perfect criminal. No one would suspect you. Are we good?"

Jim texted, "We're good, and up yours."

He pocketed his phone and listened to the hiss and cry of the baristas, then texted Sara and asked if she could meet him for lunch.

*

The MIT cafeteria resembled a train station in a medium-sized city, cavernous, with a sprawling mural high on one wall. The cafeteria was crowded, but Sara found an empty table. She seemed rushed.

"I only have thirty minutes," she said. Her tray held half a sandwich, a cup of soup, and an apple. She started eating immediately.

"Then I'll get right to it. I believe Glen Masters didn't kill Watson, but something tells me he can lead us to the killer, and that means you can help since you know him. Tell me again how well you know him."

She kept eating as she answered. "I told you all I know. My family summered near the two compounds when I was in my teens. When we started summering there, there was only one, The Greater Glory. Glen's group broke from Watson during the time we summered there."

"Before or after Watson hit on you?"

"After."

"Is that why Masters broke with Watson?"

Sara showed no affect. "No."

"You said you've seen Glen Masters a few times since then. Correct?"

"Once or twice."

"And what is your relationship now?"

"He's my stepfather."

Jim wasn't sure he heard her correctly. "Your *stepfather*? Did you say your stepfather?"

Sara shifted in her chair, as if she couldn't get comfortable. "Mom and Dad divorced after my brother died, and soon after, Mom married Masters. She was always a fundamentalist at heart."

"Why didn't you say this before?"

"I'm a private person, Judge Randall."

"On a hunch, Jim asked, "Is your mother's name Rachel?"

Sara showed surprise. "Yes, it is."

"I met her."

Sara looked shocked. "You met my mother?"

"Briefly. At the compound."

"How was she?"

"I saw her too briefly to tell. She asked if she could bring me anything to drink, then disappeared in back. Which parent did you live with after the divorce?"

"Dad, briefly. Then I went off to college and rarely saw him. Mom I never saw again. It must be twenty years."

"You were upset because she married Masters?"

"And because she devoted her life to his cause. She lost me then. I despise fundamentalism."

*

"You haven't said a word." Jim and Pat were eating dinner in his kitchen. The PBS Newshour was on.

"I'm thinking," Jim replied.

"That much is obvious. What are you thinking about?"

"How much to tell Ted and Enrique."

"Why not everything?"

"I don't want to make trouble for Sara. On the other hand, her mother being married to Masters could shed light on the murder."

"That's why you have to tell them."

"I think I'll make another visit to The Greater Good first."

The woods surrounding The Greater Good compound were thicker than he remembered and the lake not as close, although it could be glimpsed from the compound. This visit Jim had emailed Masters he was coming.

Masters greeted him at the door.

"Come inside." He ushered Jim in and gestured to the leather sofa. "My wife is not here, but can I offer you something?"

"No, thanks. Your wife is why I came."

Masters grew wary. "Is something wrong?"

"You didn't tell me last time that she is Sara Vincent's mother."

"I saw no point."

"You're lying. You were afraid to tell me."

"Why would I be afraid?"

"Stop acting. You know why."

Masters had stayed on his feet. Now he crossed the room and sat down at his computer. A few clicks later, he motioned for Jim to take a look. Over Masters's shoulder, Jim could see a beaming Rachel Masters standing in front of a wood-framed building with a sign on the door that read, "The Greater Good Girls Protective Society."

"Rachel's idea. She organized it, staffed it with members from our group, and is our liaison with the town. I'm fully on board, but it wouldn't have happened without her." Masters turned to look directly at Jim. "Now, what wrongdoing do you think this kind-hearted woman is capable of?"

Jim straightened. "I'm sure she is a fine woman, but she may be hiding something from you. Why is she estranged from Sara?"

"You apparently know, so why don't you tell me?"

"Actually, I don't. But Sara strikes me as level-headed. For her to shun her mother for so many years suggests her mother did something Sara couldn't abide."

Masters interjected, "Or maybe Sara is not as level-headed as you think. Maybe it's the other way around."

"I'll decide that for myself. In the meantime, I'd like to talk to your wife." A woman's voice over Jim's shoulder, "I'm here, Judge Randall."

Jim turned and saw Rachel Masters standing in the doorway. "Good morning, Mrs. Masters. You've been there all along, haven't you?"

"Glen and I weren't sure why you were coming. To be safe, I kept out of sight."

"Your daughter says hello."

"Did she? Did she really?" Rachel's voice had a soft center inside a serrated shell.

"It's hard for her to express emotion, but I detect concern for you. Why don't you sit down and tell me why Sara hates you so much."

Rachel took a seat next to her husband. She had a face that in repose looked very, very sad, but it didn't remain in repose for long. Unlike her daughter's impassive face, every flicker of emotion, every doubt, every fear, every fleeting hope, registered on Rachel's. Jim assessed Rachel as the kind of vulnerable person who could be driven to despair with very little provocation, and he understood how a man of certitude and rectitude like Glen Masters could seem to her to embody stability. "Sara is jealous of me. When she was in her teens, she harbored illusions that Glen would marry her when she was eighteen. When I married him, she left and never came back."

"That's hard for me to believe. Sara is too level-headed to believe in a fairy tale."

"She was as precocious as she was inexperienced, Judge Randall. Glen has told me that her advances made him uncomfortable."

"She came on to you?" Jim asked Masters, incredulously.

"I believe that is the term," Masters said.

"So the estrangement is a simple matter of jealousy?"

Rachel Masters replied, "There is nothing simple about jealousy, Judge Randall. Sara is not whom she seems. Why do you think she is so expressionless?"

"How do you know she is expressionless if you haven't seen her in years?"

Rachel nodded toward her husband. "Glen told me."

Jim looked at Masters. "You have had contact with Sara?"

"A year ago, I went down to MIT to see her. She wanted to know what she was like as a girl, when she summered near us. She seemed to be trying to clarify memories. She was searching for something, something she had lost. At least that's my interpretation."

"Anything else?"

"She asked about Melvin Watson. She mentioned the time I took her to his compound and he tried to seduce her. She asked if he was the same."

"How did you take that?"

"That she still carried a grudge against me for taking her to see Watson."

Jim was catching on; candor was not the name of Masters's game. "Another explanation for meeting Sara at MIT could be that you wanted to be alone with her. Maybe you were the one who came on to her when she was a teen, and that's why she fled. When she contacted you again to learn more about her childhood, maybe you thought she had changed her mind."

Masters didn't visibly react. "Interesting, but not true."

Jim studied them: Rachel fidgety, Glen stoic. "It seems to me you're a club of two. Okay for now, but you can't keep the world at bay forever. A murder has been committed, and the FBI is involved. God cannot protect you if you've committed a crime."

Glen broke his stoicism with a wry smile. "It's been obvious what you think of us, Judge, but I'm glad to hear you express your scorn so openly. We practice our religious beliefs quietly, in private, because it makes us feel closer to God. We have nothing to hide."

Jim rose. "Good. I shall convey that to the FBI. Mrs. Masters, is there anything you'd like me to tell Sara?"

Rachel's face reverted to its default expression, despair. She thought for a long moment. "No."

"Thanks for your time. No need to show me out." He started to go.

"Wait! There is something!" Rachel said.

Jim stopped. "Yes?"

"Tell her I'm happy. Tell her that."

Jim nodded and walked out of the house.

He pulled to the side of the road when he was away from The Greater Good and called Pat. He started to tell her what he had learned but had to pause and settle down before he could continue. Pat became alarmed.

"Jim? What's wrong? Are you okay?"

"I just left the saddest woman I have ever seen. It broke my heart. She apparently has found peace of sorts with her husband, but in the process has abandoned hope and herself."

"That's terrible."

"Yes, and she is so desperate to reconcile with her daughter, it's palpable."

"Where are you now, Jim?"

"A mile or so away from the compound. Out of the woods, literally and figuratively."

"Are you coming straight home?"

"You betcha. I shall break speed records."

5

Overnight he thought about what he had learned and in the morning arranged to meet Sara Vincent at The Long Gone.

"We could have met somewhere else, if it'd be easier for you," he said at a rear table.

"No, this is fine." Sara looked hurried.

"Isn't it out of your way?"

"Only a little. Did you see Glen?" Jim had told Sara he was going.

"Yes, and your mother. She says to tell you she is happy."

Hearing that made Sara blanch. "My mother said she is happy?"

"And that the reason for your estrangement is jealousy. You are jealous of her for marrying Glen Masters."

Sara half-turned in her chair. "That's ridiculous. Jealous?" Sara looked at the baristas doing their song and dance behind the counter. "That confirms what I've thought, that joining The Greater Good has robbed Mom of her ability to think for herself." Sara turned back to Jim. "How did she look?"

"Vulnerable. Sad. I felt sorry for her."

Sara bit her lip. A shake of her head. "Glen was a good influence at first, at least that's what I thought. But Mom didn't surrender her power of thought without someone to think for her. Now I view Glen as almost as bad as Watson, without the sexual proclivities."

"Speaking of which, she implied you made Glen uncomfortable with your attentions when you were a teenager."

"*I* made him uncomfortable?"

"Yes."

"Really? She said that? Idiotic and sad, very sad."

"Why did you go to see Masters a year ago?"

"Curiosity."

"About what?"

She became agitated. "I'm getting uncomfortable with your questions. You make me feel as if I'm on trial."

"Relax, I'm not wearing my robes. I want to know who killed Watson, that's all. So why did you go to see Glen?"

"To see if there was any hope of reconciliation with my mother."

"Why didn't you contact her directly?"

"It's none of your business." Sara drained her coffee and excused herself to get a refill. When she returned, her attitude was affectless again. "I need to get to class in a minute. If you have more questions, ask them quickly." She blew on her coffee to cool it.

"Just one. Could your mother have killed Watson?"

"With a lead pipe? Repeated blows? My mother? Don't make me laugh. The heaviest thing she ever wielded was a bible."

"She could have hired someone to kill him."

"Why would she do that? Really, Judge Randall, until now I've thought of you as sensible."

Jim replied, "And I have thought the same of you. Am I wrong?"

"I have to scoot." She gulped half her refill and stood.

"You didn't answer my question."

Sara seemed in command of herself again. "I'm more sensible than you, apparently. I've told you all I'm going to. The rest is a family matter. When we meet again, we shall discuss Kant."

"I don't like Kant."

"Then pick your philosopher, but no more family stuff."

She walked past the chirpy baristas. She walked out the door into the sunlight. He thought: she is telling the truth, but not the whole truth. If she has done no wrong, the whole truth would do no more than embarrass her, so why didn't she tell all?

The Long Gone stood still for a moment. The sensation lasted only a second, and then he realized his mind had skipped a beat and that The Long Gone was still going.

He gathered his thoughts and went outside.

Touchstones were necessary, landmarks, reference points, so get thee to the live chickens. He walked the few blocks past the mattress store and the funeral parlor and the Portugese Seaman's Society to the live poultry store. The damn chickens were still pecking at the straw, as oblivious as he was of the futility of it all. What difference did it make to his life who killed Melvin Watson? Why did he give a damn?

He kept walking until he came to Beauty Shop Row, now down to two stores, Rosie's House of Beauty and Crystal's Hair and Nails. The little nag who lived in the back of his brain told him he cared who killed Watson because of Sara Vincent. He had a soft spot for attractive women, especially brainy closed-down attractive women. Brainy closed-down women were puzzles to be solved.

He, Jim Randall, psychologist sleuth extraordinaire and debonair man about town, was just the man to solve the puzzle. But what if the solution haunted him?

All this you thought of because of Rosie's House of Beauty? Really, Jim? If he were still on the bench he would gavel his brain to order when it free-associated so crazily. Relax; Melvin Watson's murderer would be found, and Jim was sure Sara was not involved.

He was approaching the Middlesex County Courthouse, which was not long for this world, relocation being on the books, which meant relocating the prisoners who resided on the top floors (did prisoners, like nursing home residents, take a mental nosedive after being moved?). Jim was glad he had retired when he did; it would have been painful to have his bench pulled out from under him. He was close to Ted Conover's office. He stopped to report on his visit to The Greater Good.

"He's in a meeting, but he'll be out soon, if you'd care to wait, Judge."

"Thank you. I will."

The message he wanted to deliver was simple: "Glen Masters is married to Sara Vincent's mother. Sara and her mother have been estranged for years." He told this to Ted when Ted returned to his office.

"And what do you make of this?" Ted asked.

"That one of those three knows who killed Watson."

"Interesting. You've been right about a lot since you left the bench, and maybe you're right now, but my money is on a disgruntled member of Watson's cult, or a religious war between cults."

"Hell has no fury like a self-righteous cultist?"

"Something like that."

"I think I'll pay another visit to Pierre Reynolds," Jim said.

Reynolds's office in the Divinity School overlooked the construction site where Watson's body was discovered. Surrounding the construction site were a hodgepodge of buildings. No unity, no rhythm, no rhyme. Reynolds wasn't wearing a tie today, for which he apologized.

"You'll have to excuse my appearance. I'm on my way to the gym."

Jim was wearing his usual off-the-bench attire: blue shirt and khaki pants. Sometimes he varied the uniform by wearing striped blue shirts and khakis. No tie, ever. "You have me there. I don't go to the gym, and I don't wear ties."

Reynolds linked his fingers together and hid his smile behind his hands. "Did you get a chance to visit The Greater Good?"

"I did."

"And?"

"There is more than meets the eye. Masters is a guarded man, and his wife, Rachel, is an enigma. Goodness and mercy on the surface, God knows what underneath. I've visited twice. The first time they were very proper, the second very guarded. But that's not why I'm here. What do you know about other cults, if any, that feuded with Watson's group? Any long running feuds, any blood wars?"

Reynolds thought for a minute, then lowered his hands. "Plenty. Watson was hated in the fringe evangelical world. Keep in mind that no cult leader is anything other than egotistical, it goes with the territory, but Watson was considered an outlier. I'm quite sure that God's need for worship doesn't come close to Watson's. You see…" Here Reynolds stood and paced, "The hallmark of cult leaders is a massive ego that can't be satisfied in any of the traditional ways, running for office, becoming an actor, or a professor, for that matter. So what they do is surround themselves with a small group of people whose need to be led is as great as the leader's ego. It goes without saying that much of what a cult leader does is very calculated – brain-driven, not ego-driven – but the underlying drive is an insatiable need to be loved. The problem is that the insatiable need to be loved is often coupled with a capacity for cruelty." Reynolds stopped on the spot and stood stock-still. A hand went to his chin. He seemed to be reviewing his words for revision. A nod of his head, and he returned to his desk. "You want the names of the cults, I suspect."

"Please."

"I'd check out two. The One True Path, and The Devil's Enemy."

Dinner for two at Duck, Duck, Goose, thinking about The One True Path and The Devil's Enemy. Bruce with his goatee, looking slightly devilish, leading them to their table.

"I may start a cult," Jim said to Pat when they were seated. "I want to be worshipped and adored."

"I'm not surprised."

"That's not the answer I expected. Okay, if you're so smart, what was I really thinking?"

"That cults are inherently flawed, started by flawed individuals, attracting damaged people." Pat paused to gauge whether she had hit her target. "Well?"

"Nobody likes a know-it-all."

Pat tilted her head like an ingenue and smiled angelically.

"Moving on," Jim said. "Professor Reynolds gave me the names of two cults that feuded with The Greater Glory. One is based in Montana and has a dwindling long-distance feud. The other is local but has a national reputation that it's unlikely to risk by murder. But I'll check them out."

*

For help, Jim turned to Ernie Farrell, the young computer whiz Jim had defended in Jim's first foray back into court after retiring as a judge.

Ernie was living by himself after separating from his wife, Janet, whom Jim had never liked. A needier person than Janet, Jim had rarely met. Ernie's cubicle-sized apartment was across the street from a Somerville mini-mall. Jim had never been to the mall but knew where it was, since it only involved a slight deviation from his usual Beauty Shop Row/live poultry store walking route. He met Ernie at The Long Gone, as usual.

"How are you getting along?" Jim asked to start.

Ernie shrugged. "You know."

"Use words, not emoticons."

"I like being free of hassles. I hung onto the marriage too long, but I miss Janet at times, like when I face that being entirely free of hassles means being alone."

"Is there a chance you'll get back together?"

"No."

"And she agrees?"

"Whether she does or not doesn't matter. We're not getting back together." Ernie gave Jim a look. "You never liked her, did you?"

"No. I didn't think she was right for you. But I learned long ago that it's impossible to judge a marriage from the outside."

Ernie nodded and did a 360° of the coffee shop. "Well, I'll always have The Long Gone. What can I do for you?"

"I can google as well as the next guy, but I don't understand the intricacies of the internet. You do. Can you research two cults for me?"

"What are their names?"

"The One True Path, and The Devil's Enemy."

"You've gotta be kidding. Are you sure they aren't video games?"

"There you go, ideas for your next app. You can thank me later."

Jim had not seen anything about Watson's death in the press since the initial flurry of stories. Sasha Cohen, who had helped him in the Wilcox case, was now with the *Boston Globe* and might know more. He called her.

"We haven't talked in a long time," she said. He had a minor crush on her when she was helping him. He had minor crushes on almost all the young women he met since he emerged from his long mourning about Joyce, but none of the women had anything to fear since he was ancient and loyal to Pat. Minor crushes with the young were a way of reliving his youth – actually, his youth had stunk much of the time – okay, crushes with the young were his way of living the youth he never had. No matter, no harm done, and Sasha was fine, she said.

"Are you at liberty to tell me if your Spotlight Team is doing background reporting on the Watson murder?" he asked.

"Not as far as I know," she replied. "I can find out."

"Would you?"

"Can't stay away from the action, can you, Jim?"

"I didn't volunteer. I was invited. I was on a panel with Watson just before he died."

"I heard. You have a way about you."

"Stay away, should be a warning sign I wear."

"How have you been?" Sasha asked.

"I've been fine. Really fine. Pat and I are happy." "You and Kent?"

"Still a pair. For now."

"Trouble?"

"Not at all. Not everything has to be forever."

"Why not? Why can't things hold still?"

"You sound like my father."

"Stop it."

She chuckled. "I'll get back to you. Good to talk to you, Jim."

After he hung up he had another thought: minor crushes with the young were a way of thumbing his nose at death.

"I am very wise," he announced to Pat as they were reading in bed.

"You've always said."

"Am I jeopardizing our safety by dabbling in murder?"

"I think you are invincible."

"No, seriously. Are you afraid?"

"As judges we tried cases which frightened us, and we've been through a lot in the relatively short time we've been a couple. So the answer is no."

"You don't want me to quit the detective business?"

"Would you, if I asked you to?"

Jim thought about that. "I don't know."

"Anyway, I'd never ask, I know you too well. Keep in mind I was by your side when Hawkins kidnapped us, and I'm still with you."

"Actually, the first time we made love was the night he freed us. Remember?"

"Was that you? Just kidding. Yes, I remember. No, I don't want you to quit your newfound hobby. You'd be bored, and you'd make me miserable."

Sasha Cohen called Jim back the next morning. "*The Globe* Spotlight Team is not investigating Melvin Watson or The Greater Glory, but I just learned from our police desk that a suspect in Watson's murder has been arrested."

"Any details?"

"Not yet. The report just came through."

Jim hung up and called Ted. Before he could explain the call, Ted said, "I guess you heard. We have a suspect."

"I did. Just heard. Who is he?"

"A homeless person. Cambridge Police got an anonymous tip of a heated argument behind the Divinity School the night of the murder. The suspect is known to the police. He has a history of violence when he is off his meds. The anonymous caller didn't see the fatal blows but did see and hear a lot of pushing, shoving, and shouting. The FBI is involved because of the possible hate crime angle, but the preliminary conclusion is that this was a random act of violence."

When Jim didn't respond, Ted questioned, "You have doubts?"

"Plenty. Too easy and tidy a conclusion. Who is going to vouch for a homeless man? Perfect scapegoat. No, there is too much bad blood in the world of cults for the murder to be random."

"Would you feel differently if you knew the suspect admitted getting angry at a man who fit Watson's description? He claims the man refused to give him money and cursed him for giving in to the temptation of alcohol, said he had fallen into the devil's trap."

"Anger and murder are two different things."

"They aren't necessarily far apart in this case because of the suspect's history of sudden, explosive rages. He claims he hadn't been drinking heavily that night. He took offense at the devil's name, said he is a believer in God and a good Christian, in spite of his drinking problem."

"Any forensic evidence that implicates him?"

"His fingerprints on the pipe."

"He could've picked up the pipe after it was used to kill Watson. Fingerprints aren't the gold standard anymore, as you know."

"The police and FBI are checking into all of this. For the time being, we're holding the guy."

"Will you let me talk to him?"

"Not now, Jim. If he's booked and is willing to talk to you, maybe."

An anonymous tip. A homeless guy. Too convenient. Jim didn't believe a word.

He walked to The Long Gone to clear his head.

It was very strange for him to experience law enforcement as a civilian. There was more luck involved than he had thought, more approximations. By the time a case reached court, the questions had been narrowed. A judge is presented with limited choices, not a blank slate. Now, walking to The Long Gone and wondering if a homeless man, an angry cult member, or a murderer to be named later was the culprit, the options seemed limitless and therefore daunting.

A 69 bus pulled to the curb inches from Jim, startling him. Damn buses.

The Long Gone was emptier than usual. He ordered a dark roast at the counter and sat at a front table – he preferred the rear of the dark room for privacy but decided he ought to try the front while opportunity knocked. A front table at The Long Gone. Is there no end to the changes a retired judge is willing to make?

Too near the front door, he decided after a few minutes at the table. Bursts of light when the door opened. Never again. Too distracting.

His phone dinged. A text from Ernie. "I have the info you wanted. When and where?"

Jim texted back. "I am at The Long Gone. Meet me here?"

"In 15."

Ernie's report, delivered breathlessly, cleared The One True Path. "A handful of followers in Montana, led by an 87-year-old man on his last legs. As his health has failed, his followers have drifted away. There are only a handful left."

"What about The Devil's Enemy?"

"More likely. Located in the Berkshires, a tight-knit group of true believers who live in town and involve themselves in town government. All of the group's material on the web is mainstream Christianity. Only when I dug down did a find some quirky stuff."

"Such as?"

"A possible link to a porn site that skirts the law on the depiction of minors, judging by what I saw. If you believe you are doing God's work, you can justify everything you do."

"Wonderful, sex and God again. Who is the leader?"

"A man named Ulysses Taylor. Served time for assault and battery and possession. After he did his time, his story of personal redemption resonated with the fallen and, voila, he had himself a cult. His Twitter feed was full of anti-Watson vitriol until Watson died."

"Was the vitriol between Taylor and Watson a two-way street?"

"Very much so. They hated each other. My guess is they appealed to the same constituency and saw each other as natural enemies. If you're thinking of visiting Taylor, be careful. He's a bad dude."

Jim went back to Pierre Reynolds with the new information. "What do you know about Ulyssess Taylor?"

"Bad dude. I'd stay away if I were you."

*

Jim was better at giving advice than taking it. The town of Hidden Falls, a two-and-a-half-hour drive west of

Boston, was overshadowed by the surrounding hills. Jim pulled up at the general store and inquired inside about Ulysses Taylor.

"Never heard of him. Don't know him," the visibly rattled clerk answered.

"Really? I heard he had influence in town."

"You heard wrong, mister. You gonna buy anything?"

Main Street was three blocks long, and Jim chose to walk its length when he left the store. Tidy houses, cracked sidewalks. He was approaching one stately house when a large man emerged and approached Jim. The man filled the sidewalk and gave no indication of moving aside. He stopped a few feet in front of Jim.

"Why are you trying to find me?"

"Ulysses Taylor?"

The man was six feet five, with a wide face and fixed frown. "Who are you?"

"Judge Randall. Pleased to meet you."

"You're a judge?"

"Retired."

"What do you want from me?"

"I could be seeking salvation, have you thought of that?"

"How did you hear about me?"

"So far you have answered all of my questions with a question. Why I'm here is to find out if you hated Melvin Watson enough to kill him. Your turn."

Taylor looked as if he might smile. Instead, his mouth stretched like a rubber band and snapped back to a frown. "No, I didn't hate Melvin Watson enough to kill him. There, I gave you an answer."

"Did you kill him for reasons other than hatred?"

Taylor asked, "Which way are you walking?"

"Whichever way you are."

"I'm going into town."

"We aren't already in it?"

"I mean downtown. The general store."

"Where they don't know you."

"We are very protective of each other in this town."

"I can confirm that. Why so protective?"

"Too many people come to town looking for the zoo animals. That's us, The Devil's Enemy. Freaks, fanatics. We're not freaks or fanatics, we just like our religion strong and straight."

"With a dash of child porn?"

Taylor stopped walking. His voice became a freight train. "If you weren't so old, I'd beat your fucking brains out."

"Don't let my age stop you, if you enjoy that sort of thing."

Taylor resumed walking. "Not worth it." A moment passed. "If you were a judge you ought to realize I would never kill Watson because I'm such an obvious suspect. Watson was a charlatan and a pervert, but I didn't kill him. Besides, I have an alibi. I was hosting new recruits at my house when he died."

"Somebody killed him for you?"

"Not anybody in my group. They're all peaceable people, I'm the only hothead." They reached the general store. "By the way, the FBI beat you to me. I told them the same thing I've told you. Coming in?"

"No, I have all I need. Say goodbye to the store clerk for me and introduce yourself to him while you're at it."

Jim was closer to his Vermont house than to Cambridge, so he stayed overnight on his hillside. In the morning the light over the valley made him wonder why he wasted time on murder. He checked in with Pat before his drive home.

"A night's sleep hasn't changed my opinion. Taylor's an entrepreneur, not a murderer. He controls his town and his porn site brings in cash. Why risk it all?"

6

Which left Jim back at square one. The homeless man.

"His story checks out, Jim," Ted told him the next time they met. "He was sleeping behind the Divinity School when Watson shook him awake. At first Watson was solicitous, said he was a man of God who wanted to help, then turned hostile and accusatory. The suspect claims Watson shoved him, the suspect pushed back, and that led to a struggle that left Watson lying unconscious in the ditch. The suspect admits hitting him in the head with the pipe."

"He confessed to the murder?" Jim said.

"No. He swears that he hit Watson in self-defense and that Watson was alive when he fled."

"Any way to confirm or deny that?"

"Not yet. We're working on it."

"A dead evangelist, the lead pipe, in the ballroom."

"Excuse me?"

"Never mind."

His next stop was Sara Vincent's office. She didn't seem delighted to see him. "Still think my mother did it?"

"Mind if I sit down?"

"Please. If you can be civil."

Sara's office befitted a Stoic. Desk, two chairs, whiteboard on the wall. He pulled his chair closer to her desk.

"No, I don't think your mother did it. And I don't think the homeless man did it, either."

"But the police have charged him." She seemed agitated, although with Sara it was hard to tell.

"I think the police are wrong."

"So, who killed Watson?"

"What do you think?"

She stood, visibly agitated. "I'm supposed to know? How am I supposed to know? You're the know-it-all."

"Easy, Sara. It was a question, not an accusation. I've checked out a couple of other cults that might have wanted Watson out of the way. So far, no luck. The murder happened between the end of the panel and the early morning hours. Pat and I walked you partway home that night. Did you see or hear anything out of the ordinary as you passed the Divinity School?"

"No, nothing. I got home at ten or so, and went straight to bed."

"Has anything new come into your head about Glen Masters or Melvin Watson or their cults that might shed light? Anything from the summers when your family stayed near the compounds?"

"No. Dad was a piano teacher. During the school year he taught music at our high school, and in summers gave lessons to a few kids from the two Greaters. I remember him complaining that he couldn't teach a kid who was only allowed to listen to religious music. He had little use for God, didn't deny Him, just had no interest in Him. Mom was a different story, she wanted so badly to believe but hadn't found a religion that fulfilled her needs. Watson appealed to her at first but later seemed extreme even to her. Mom needed certainty in her life, but Watson went too far. Then, when Masters parted from Watson, Mom had found her guru. She kept it quiet at first because Dad didn't understand. By the time she told Dad, it was too late to save the marriage."

"And you resented your mother. Is that why you chose to live with your father after the divorce?"

"That, and the fact that music seemed to me a truer calling than religion. We weren't going to talk about my family, remember?"

"I remember. One more question, please, then we'll talk about Seneca." Jim thought he detected a smile.

"Not Kant?" Sara said.

"I hate Kant, I told you."

"One more question, and that's all."

"Where is your father now?"

"He lives in one room in the South End. He's eighty-three. He still teaches piano, although he left the high school long ago."

"He's much older than your mother."

"Twenty-five years. I think that's one reason Mom married him. An older man who was set in his ways gave her the certainty she needed."

"Do you see him?"

"Not often. That's his choice, he is most comfortable alone. You said one question. That's two."

"You're right. On to Seneca. Did he furnish your office?"

Sara laughed. An actual laugh. No pursing of the lips to squelch it, no swallowing of the breath to mute it. A laugh. "I relied on a range of Hellenistic thinkers, all of whom believed that pleasure was best achieved by avoiding unnecessary frills like decoration."

"Not even a picture on the wall?"

A final, dwindling laugh. The last bounce of a ball. "Especially not a picture."

"Sara, would you introduce me to your father?"

"Why would you want to meet him?"

"To round out the picture. To help me understand the context of Watson's murder."

Her face became concrete. "Never. And don't keep asking. I know you well enough to know you are a persistent man, but you know by now that I mean what I say. I intend to keep Dad out of this. Mom hurt him badly when she left him and questioning him now would add to his pain."

*

Pat cooked a quick dinner at her place that night. Jim was so preoccupied he barely noticed what he ate. "I can't figure Sara out. When she lets down her guard, she gives the impression of having nothing to hide. But then she shuts tight. Is she hiding something, or is that just her way?"

"My impression is that she is a person who was badly hurt in childhood and erected defenses that even she can't penetrate."

"Trapped by her own defenses." Jim pointed with his fork. "What am I eating?"

"Fish."

"Oh."

"Do you like it?"

"I liked it more when I didn't know it was fish. I think you are on to something. Sara put herself in solitary confinement for safe keeping and forgot where she put the key."

"Where does that leave you?" Pat said.

"Probably nowhere. Sara's not the villain, but what works for me is learning as much as I can about everyone involved, and Sara is very much involved."

Jim awoke the next morning with the homeless man on his mind. At a decent hour he called Ted. "What do you know about the suspect in the Watson murder?"

"Sad story, but not atypical for a man who has lived on the street for a dozen years. He had a wife, a job, and a drinking problem. She left him, he drank more, lost his job and his home. Borderline schizophrenic. Violent when aroused, otherwise docile. Sleeps in the cluster of buildings behind the Divinity School. The ongoing construction opened up a wealth of new hiding places. He is well known to the Harvard Police."

"What kind of work did he do?"

"His name is Dexter Hutchins. And get this, Dexter Hutchins was a researcher in the human genome. His focus was the brain. A brilliant man, once upon a time."

"He admits hitting Watson with the pipe?"

"His memory is hazy, but he remembers an argument that became physical, which he thinks ended with him hitting Watson with the pipe."

"He thinks that, but isn't sure?"

"As time passes, he's less sure."

"Has he been assigned a lawyer?"

"Of course. Do you have anything new?"

"Nothing crucial. I'll let you know."

One person Jim hadn't looked into was Richie Monroe, the super-rich techie who financially propped up The Greater Glory when it was in trouble. Where to find him? Kendall Square was the new Silicon Valley. Ernie might have heard of him.

"Richie Monroe? Yes, I've heard of him. Considered the next Steve Jobs until he gave money to The Greater Glory. Happens a lot in the tech world. Guys who are good with gadgets go off the deep end when they venture outside their comfort zone. Because they are visionaries in tech they think they are visionaries in everything."

"What is he doing now?" Jim and Ernie were sitting at The Long Gone. The before-work crowd was sluggish. Shuffle to your seat with your latte and think of how to save the world with an app.

"After Monroe grew disillusioned with The Greater Glory, he started a company devoted to finding technological answers to hunger. He's got about six people huddled in a room. He's been quoted as saying that six good brains coupled to computers can be smarter than a thousand ordinary people."

"Mr. Humility."

"Sounds arrogant, I know. But guys like Monroe think they're just being honest, and they see nothing arrogant about honesty."

"Where is he located?"

"Kendall Square. Near the T."

"I'm going to pay him a visit. Want to join me?"

"I'm just a humble programmer."

"And I'm just a humble retired judge. Come with me."

Richie Monroe said he would be glad to receive them. He seemed to welcome any chance to talk about his work.

The office resembled a college common room before most of the furniture has been delivered. A few couches, a table or two, and more empty pizza boxes than monitors. Monroe looked eighteen, although he was in his early thirties.

"We believe that computers can solve problems that humans can't. Computers have no emotions, that's their advantage," Monroe said, his face alight.

"Aren't computers told what to do by humans?"

"Yes, for now. Eventually it will be the other way around."

"As interesting as your work is, we came to talk about your philanthropy, specifically your support of The Greater Good."

Monroe corrected Jim. "My *former* support, I stopped giving months ago."

"What prompted you to give in the first place? A fundamentalist religion seems antithetical to your work."

"I explored religion to see what I was missing, and Melvin Watson impressed me at first. He was a charismatic man."

"I would've thought you were immune to charisma."

"Precisely because I lack it, I was charmed when I encountered it in Watson."

"And what made you change your mind?"

"The way he treats women is abominable. I'm gay so it's not personal with me, but really? Fourteen-year-olds? Reading his material online, I had no idea. Only when I spent time at his compound did I understand."

"Doesn't that show the limits of computers? You needed human interaction to unmask him."

Monroe shrugged. "Computer science is still in its infancy." He turned to Ernie. "You are a programmer?"

"I am. I write code for games."

Monroe didn't seem put off by that. "Games can be a high form of intelligence." He turned back to Jim. "Who killed Reverend Watson, do you think?"

"I don't know yet. The police arrested a suspect, but his motive seems thin."

"It was horrible, what happened to Watson. Dead in a ditch. No one deserves to die like that, not even Watson. You were on the panel with him, weren't you? I saw the clip on YouTube."

"I was. He orchestrated it. He grabbed me to grab headlines. Where were you that night?"

"Where I always am. Here. With Ralph and Jessie, if you want to ask them." Monroe gestured to two co-workers.

"That won't be necessary. While you were involved with The Greater Good, did you meet anyone in the group who might want to kill Watson?"

"I'm sure he turned a lot of stomachs besides mine. But I didn't get to know his followers well enough to know who the disgruntled ones might be. Watson was a master at keeping his followers in silos. Anything else? My attention span is depleted."

As Jim and Ernie walked to the Red Line, Jim asked for Ernie's impressions of Monroe. Ernie replied, "Guys like him are going to rule the world, and that scares the hell out of me. But he didn't kill Watson. I know how minds like his work. Why resort to murder when technology can solve all problems?"

"Did he hire someone else to do it?"

Ernie thought that over. "Possible, but I doubt it. Guys like Monroe wash their hands of disappointment and move on to the next project. That's one advantage to having a piece missing from your personality, you don't take things personally."

*

Jim read Cicero that evening in Pat's living room. The living room had the feel of a library, and he liked reading in it more than in his living room, though not as much as reading in his study. Cicero was a man of enormous ego; a gifted orator, a statesman, and later in life, a philosopher. Early in his career, he was renowned as a lawyer and tried a number of prominent murder cases.

Jim lowered his book to think. Glen Masters? A disgruntled member of The Greater Glory? The suspect, Dexter Hutchins?

Who had the most incentive to kill Watson? Not Hutchins. A disgruntled member of The Greater Glory, perhaps, or Glen Masters, who had broken with Watson and become his fierce enemy.

Jim decided to revisit The Greater Good, but this time he would ask Sara to go with him.

She resisted his invitation, to say the least. "Absolutely not."

"You need to settle things with your mother, Sara."

"Why?"

"Do you intend never to see her again?"

"I haven't thought that far ahead."

"If one of you died right now, you wouldn't want to end on this note. I'll be honest with you, I also hope seeing you will pry your mother or Masters out of their protective shells."

7

The weather was cool, the sky clear, the morning Jim and Sara drove to Maine. Jim would prefer to be driving to Vermont, if truth were told. Having decided to come, Sara seemed preternaturally calm.

She hadn't decided immediately, but Jim had come to understand her thought process, adamant at first, dropping the subject for days, then deciding quickly and decisively. A lot like his thought process. Duck, dawdle, decide.

"What's your strategy?" she asked halfway to The Greater Good.

"No strategy. Play it by ear."

"Doesn't that scare you?"

"It used to. No more. I've become the soul of flexibility."

Sara didn't laugh or smile. Why react visibly, she must be thinking; save your emoting for when it counts.

They drove into the compound in mid-morning. Glen and Rachel Masters did not expect them.

"Nervous?" Jim asked.

"What does my mother look like now?"

"Tired. Sad. I don't know what she looked like before."

They pulled up in front of the Masters's cottage and got out. Rachel Masters answered the door.

When she saw Jim, she asked with some heat, "What do you want now? Haven't you caused enough trouble?"

Then she saw Sara and gasped.

"Hello, Mother."

Rachel Masters backed away from the door. Sara stepped forward. "May we come in?"

"What do you want?"

"To see you. To say hello to my stepfather."

"He's not here."

Jim said, "May we come in anyway, Mrs. Masters?"

She let them pass. She looked as if she might faint. They entered the room and sat on the sofa. Rachel perched at the table where Glen had his computer.

Rachel recovered her composure. Her habitual sad expression returned. "After all these years, I'm surprised to see you, Sara."

"Being here surprises me too. I haven't forgiven you, but neither of us is getting younger."

"You look the same," Rachel said.

"No, I don't. And neither do you."

Jim spoke, "Mrs. Masters, you may have heard that the police arrested a suspect in Glen Watson's murder."

"I hadn't. I don't follow the news, only the Lord. Is the suspect a member of The Greater Glory?"

"No, he's a homeless man in Cambridge, once a brilliant scientist, probably mentally ill."

"Why did he kill Melvin?"

"Schizophrenic rage is the official explanation. I'm not sure that's the whole story."

"So that's why you're here?"

"To find out more. Yes. And I'll be blunt. The last time I was here, I was struck by how palpable your yearning to see your daughter was."

Rachel turned away in embarrassment. "I don't think of you as a sentimental man, Judge Randall."

"I'm usually not. This is an extreme case."

"Are you happy, Mother?" Sara asked.

"Praise the Lord."

"Is that a yes?"

"Happiness is His to bestow. I count myself lucky."

"Jim has told me you help teenage girls in the village."

"Poor creatures. They need guidance."

"The same way you helped me?" Sara's voice didn't change inflection but Rachel recoiled in horror.

"You raise that now, after all these years? How dare you?"

Jim thought fast. He had no idea what they were talking about, but it was clearly an explosive issue. Let them continue or change the subject? "Will your husband be back soon? I'd like to talk to him."

Glad for the diversion, Rachel said, "He crossed the border. I don't know when he'll be back."

"The border?"

"Between The Greater Good and The Greater Glory. He's gone to the other side frequently since Watson was killed."

"Did he before?"

"Never."

Sara addressed Jim. "I'd like to speak to my mother alone. Do you mind?"

"Not at all. I'll wait in the car."

"We won't be long," Rachel Masters said.

Jim got up to go. "Take your time."

The outdoor air smelled good. Not as good as in Vermont, but better than Cambridge. Something very disturbing had just taken place, and he didn't know what it was.

Jim went to his car but realized he was too agitated to sit still. So he walked, aimlessly at first, then towards what he perceived as the border between the communes. He half-expected to encounter World War I trenches and submachine guns, but the only demarcation of the border was a long rope, which could easily be mistaken as a clothesline if one didn't know better. There were no people in sight on either side of the border. He crossed over from the Good to the Glory, wondering if God could tell the difference.

The cottages on the Glory side looked much like the cottages on the Good side. As small as trailers. Two dozen or more, on each side of an open space. On each side, the dwellings were arrayed in a circle with the leader's cottage the anchor; wagon trains in the early West.

He walked into the center of the circle on the Glory side, still no people in sight.

He stood in the middle and called, "Hello! Anybody here?"

Several doors opened at once. Glen Masters emerged from one and approached him. "What are you doing here?" Masters's tone seemed demanding yet not hostile.

"Looking for you, among other things. And exploring, as is my wont."

The other people who appeared in doorways (all of them men except for one young woman) looked at Jim as if they didn't know whether to be curious or frightened.

"Let's go back to where I feel comfortable," Masters said.

"No. I want to meet some of these people."

Masters firmly grasped Jim's arm and started walking. "They don't take kindly to outsiders. If you want to ask them questions, you can do it via me."

"Since when are you their leader?"

"I'm not, but at least they know me."

Jim allowed himself to be led. Resistance would frighten these people. As he and Masters walked to the border, Jim asked, "Is that why you've been coming over to this side, to collect followers?"

"To give the lost a safe haven. They are without a leader, they who need a leader more than life itself."

"Which gives you a motive for murder."

They came to the rope which marked the border. Masters lifted it so he and Jim could duck under. "I guess so."

"You're not concerned?"

"I didn't kill him. I was at home when it happened. Am I glad he's dead? You bet I am, he was evil. But did I kill him? Again, I say an emphatic no."

"How convenient that the people who had motive to murder Watson deny any role, while the only person who admits a role is a man who had no motive."

They reached Masters's house and went in. Sara was sitting alone in the living room.

"Where's Rachel?" Masters demanded.

"She was upset. She went to her bedroom."

Masters hurried to the back of the house.

Jim asked Sara what happened. Stonefaced, Sara shrugged. A few minutes later, Masters stormed out and confronted Sara. "What have you done to my wife?"

"You have the question backwards. It should be, what has she done to me?"

"Get out! Both of you! Now!"

In the car driving away, Jim demanded, "What happened between you and your mother while I was gone?"

"It doesn't involve you. A private matter."

"If it involves Watson's murder, it's not a private matter."

"It doesn't. Please, Jim, let me have some secrets."

Maine slid by. Villages, shallow valleys, then seacoast. The Greater Glory and The Greater Good already seemed in the distant past. Sara was silent until they approached Cambridge.

Jim broke her silence with a question. "Are you glad you came?"

She glanced at Jim. "I should have gone earlier. Some things needed to be said. Did *you* get what you wanted from the trip?"

"Masters is clearly taking advantage of Watson's death to increase his flock which gives him motive, but he says he was at home and I'll bet Rachel will confirm it. So I don't have answers yet, just more questions."

"The killer may be Dexter Hutchins, after all. Will you be disappointed if it is?"

"Disappointed? No. But you are perceptive, I don't like to be wrong. How about you?"

Her expression didn't change. "I'm never wrong."

He couldn't tell if she were joking. He let her off at her house. A tidy two-family in a tight-knit neighborhood. "I'll let you know if I hear anything," he said.

She nodded and slid out of the car. He waited until she had unlocked her front door, then drove the short distance home.

8

The idea came to Jim's mind two nights later while he was eating alone at Duck, Duck, Goose. Jim often ate alone at the horseshoe counter before he and Pat became a couple.

"Miss me?" he asked Chris, the counterman/sommelier.

"I could hardly stand it. How have you been?"

"Confused. Befuddled."

Chris whisked a bottle from under the counter and poured Jim a glass. "On the house, Judge."

"What is it?"

"Tell me if you like it, then I'll tell you."

Jim swirled, sniffed, and tasted. Earthy, with overtones of worm. His nose must have wrinkled because Chris said, "Don't like it, huh?"

"What the hell is it?"

"A Madiran." Chris showed him the label.

"Give it to your horses with their hay."

Chris snatched Jim's glass away. "Try this." He put another glass in front of Jim. Jim smiled.

"Côtes du Rhône, right?"

"Has anyone ever told you you are a fuddy-duddy?"

"Not in those words, which I didn't know someone your age knew. Now leave me alone and let me think."

Chris smiled. "Welcome back, Judge."

Jim emptied his mind of nagging worries and everyday concerns, and reviewed what he knew and what he didn't. Why couldn't he accept that Dexter Hutchins was Watson's killer? Was it because Hutchins's recall was so hazy? Or was it simply because a schizophrenic drunk was too easy a scapegoat?

Jim recalled what he felt when he crossed the border to The Greater Glory. An eerie, haunting stillness. Seeing no one until men and a woman appeared at their doors in unison like zombies – the members of The Greater Glory had been watching him from their windows, that much was clear. Were they so afraid of outsiders?

Perhaps because the image was so disturbing, his mind zoomed to Harriet, an attractive woman he had met at this very counter before he took up with Pat. He had invited her over to his house for a drink, where she helped him accept Joyce's death, for which he was grateful, but nothing came of it. And then he thought of Pat, how lucky he was to have worked with her, gotten to know her slowly, before they became a couple. How lucky he was, how blessed.

Enough diversions. Who killed Watson?

Duck, Duck, Goose was especially lively that night, more laughter than usual, less academic cant. Jim listened to the convivial buzz for a moment, then concluded for one last time that his focus from now on should be the nexus of Sara, her mother, and Glen Masters. The tension in the Masters's house when he and Masters returned to find Sara alone in the living room had been painful. Something disturbing had occurred between Sara and her mother while he and Masters were at The Greater Glory, something that reopened old wounds.

He wanted Ted and Enrique to hear about his visit. Enrique was the first to have an opening in his schedule.

"Glen Masters has taken advantage of Watson's death to recruit members from The Greater Glory."

"And you think that is motive for murder or you wouldn't be telling me."

"I don't think Dexter Hutchins's confession tells the whole story, and I think the rest of the story will be found at The Greater Good or The Greater Glory."

"Do you think a member of one of those cults is the killer?"

"Not necessarily. But I think one of members knows the answer."

"Intriguing. For now, the FBI has no reason to stay involved. The police have a confession and no concrete evidence contradicts it. We have turned the matter over to the DA."

"I'm seeing Ted next."

"If you learn anything that might prompt us to reopen our investigation, let me know."

Ted Conover was ending a trial, and Jim had to wait to see him. He looked worn out, his eyes sunk deep in their sockets.

"You okay?" Jim asked.

"Nothing's wrong with me that a vacation wouldn't cure."

"Any on the horizon?"

"Not until the illegal campaign financing trial and the sex trafficking trial are finished. Something new on the Watson murder?"

Jim told him about his visit to The Greater Good.

"Jim, I think the world of you, but your suspicions don't trump a confession."

"Has Hutchins's memory gotten any better? Does he remember the full sequence of events?"

"Not really. But you know that memory can be sketchy, especially when someone is in a schizophrenic rage. Hutchins has a history of violent outbursts, his fingerprints are on the pipe, and he confesses to hitting Watson over the head with it." Ted shrugged as if to say, "What else do you want from me?"

"Keep an open mind, Ted, that's all I ask. And take some time off. I'm worried about you."

Ted nodded thanks.

Jim wanted to touch base with Sara. It had been over a week since their trip and they hadn't talked, but she didn't want to see him. "I'm done with murder, Jim. I had a very nice life before Watson's death, and I will have a very nice life again once I put the murder out of my mind."

"Are you sorry I took you to see your mother?"

"No. It was painful but necessary. I should have done it long ago. I'm grateful you insisted."

He hesitated. "Sara, I know you well enough to know *I* can't change your mind but if you change your mind, I'm here. And I still hate Kant."

She chuckled. "You're an idiot."

"Are we still friends?"

"Don't push your luck. Yes, we're friends. And maybe someday I'll tell you the whole story about my mother."

*

George Barrows, the Divinity School dean, greeted Jim warmly. "How have you been? What have you learned?"

"Let me answer with a question. Are there degrees of cult-like behavior among cults? Are some more extreme than others?"

"Definitely. Some turn their followers into automatons, some are simply tighter versions of a fraternity or sorority. Why?"

"Funny you should use the word automaton. I visited The Greater Glory and that describes the people I glimpsed."

"They let you into their compound?"

"I entered via the rear door, so to speak. Glen Masters took me there. He is poaching members from The Greater Glory for his group."

Barrows swiveled in his chair and looked out the window at the construction site. He swiveled back to face Jim.

"Tell Pierre about this, will you? He's our cult guy."

"I plan to see him next. Did you know how extreme Watson was when you invited him to be on the panel?"

"Not really. Sara Vincent suggested him because he was at the one end of the spectrum, she being at the other. You were in the middle. She thought it would make for an interesting panel."

"I see."

"Am I to infer from your continuing interest that you have doubts that the police have Watson's killer?"

"I have doubts that we know the full story."

Barrows reflected. "I studied religion because it asks questions that science and philosophy can't answer, but when I see religion being used to excuse aberrant behavior, I lose heart. I'm tired of people who use religion for selfish purposes, who hide behind God like children hiding behind their mothers' skirts."

The dean paused in his reflections. "I'm glad I made the choice to study religions. I still believe in a divinity, but I want a dose of humility with my divinity."

Pierre Reynolds was teaching a class when Jim left the dean's office, so Jim walked. Jim liked North Cambridge but felt more comfortable in Mid-Cambridge. The stretch of Mass Ave north of Harvard Square seemed part of Harvard; the stretch of Cambridge Street between Harvard and Inman Squares seemed like part of a city. He stopped for coffee at a pizza shop.

Give it up, Jim heard himself say. Call it quits. The Greater Glory and The Greater Good had provided pleasant diversion. In the process he had learned about cults. But you are in over your head this time. A journeyman ex-judge was no match for – in the dean's formulation – those who hide behind God like children hiding behind their mothers' skirts.

A calm mind. That's what he would gain if he stopped kidding himself that he could solve this case. Heed the dean, seek answers to the big questions, not to who killed Melvin Watson.

He made it to Porter Square before his legs gave out. Strange, he usually didn't tire when walking – his upper body strength was a joke, but his legs were strong. He rode the long escalator down past the sculptured gloves to the Red Line and got on the train to Harvard Square, feeling tired and defeated.

At the last minute – as the doors opened – he decided to stay on the T. He got off at Charles Street and walked up Beacon Hill to Pat's.

Now that she had finished the memoir, or at least a first draft, she was busying herself with civic causes and was home less often, but Jim had a house key. He let himself in and his resolve returned. Like magic.

Though Joyce's companionship had consistently been a pleasure, it had never been a building block, like Pat's was. Late in life was not too late, he realized, which strengthened his resolve: find Watson's killer, seek answers to the big questions, and spend time with Pat. Your life in a capsule. Take twice a day, with food. See your doctor if the symptoms don't go away.

By the time Pat got home, Jim felt ten years younger. Pat noticed right away. "What have you been up to?"

"Chasing young chicks."

"Any success?"

"Like you wouldn't believe. Why do I feel compelled to get involved in cases that are none of my business?"

"Because you once were a judge who held peoples' fate in your hands, and you can't give up the habit."

*

Pierre Reynolds had just returned from the gym and was still wearing sweats. "I hope you don't mind meeting this early, but I have classes all day."

"I'm an early riser."

"Do you work out?"

"Walking is my exercise and my meditation."

Reynolds smiled. "I play squash. Sometimes I win. What's this in your message about visiting The Greater Glory?"

"Yes, I swam the Rio Grande, so to speak. Eerie emptiness, no people in sight at first, no barking dogs. I called hello and doors opened in unison and people appeared, Glen Masters being one. Masters is poaching members from The Greater Glory now that Watson is dead. Does that surprise you?"

"Cult leaders are aware of each other. They limit their members' access to knowledge but they know everything about each other and have been known to raid each other's membership. But the rivalry between The Greater Glory and The Greater Good was an extreme case, because of the proximity and the personal animus between Watson and Masters."

"Have there been cases of murder between cults?"

"Not that I'm aware of."

"So there's nothing about being a true believer that engenders violence?"

"I didn't say that. You asked a specific question. True believers are guilty of all manner of bad behavior, including slaughter of innocents, but The Greater Glory and The Greater Good do not have a history of violence. A history of histrionics, yes."

"Are any ex-members of The Greater Glory living in the Boston area?"

"I interviewed a former member for a paper I planned to write. Angela Butler."

Angela Butler was a night student at Bunker Hill Community College. She reluctantly agreed to meet Jim.

She worked at a clothing store during the day. They met at a bar on Newbury Street.

She was an open-faced woman with eyes that said keep away. Jim guessed her to be in her mid-twenties.

"Thanks for meeting with me," he said joining her at the bar.

"Professor Reynolds said I can trust you. He said you were a judge."

"Was a judge. I'm retired now."

"Professor Reynolds said you visited The Greater Glory."

"That's correct."

"How did it seem? Did you talk to anyone?"

"Desolate. No, I didn't, in fact I didn't see anyone at first."

"I miss it in a way. My mother is still there."

"I only saw one woman, and she was too young to be your mother."

She nodded. "It's wrong to speak ill of the dead, but Melvin Watson was evil. He deserved to die. He repeatedly abused me starting when I was twelve. He claimed that since he was a messenger of God, having sex with him meant I was serving the Lord. I didn't believe him, but I was too scared to do anything about it, and my mother wanted me to do whatever pleased him. She worshiped him."

"Did you feel abandoned?"

Her face expressed surprise. "Totally. The only people who understood how I felt were the other girls he abused."

"There were many?"

"Oh, yes."

"You were brave to leave."

"It was hard, very hard. I stopped believing Watson's words long ago, but he was a very powerful man, and since I never knew my father, Watson seemed like a father to me, until he did what he did."

"Why didn't you go to the police after you broke away?"

"I did."

"And?"

"The police visited the compound and found no one else willing to file a complaint, and that was the last I heard of it."

"I take it you haven't been back to the compound since you left."

"Never. I may one day, now that he's gone."

"Did you ever think about killing him?"

"Many times. I left instead."

"Do you think someone else he abused killed him?"

She shook her head. "He took over our minds so thoroughly I doubt anyone would have the will power to kill him. It was hard enough to break away. Sorry, I have to get to class."

"I'm grateful to you for talking to me. I hope I haven't caused you pain. Here is my card in case you want to contact me."

Jim was rattled by what he had heard. When he left the bar he couldn't face the T so he walked down Newbury Street, a street of expensive clothing stores and trendy restaurants. He couldn't imagine what is was like for Angela Butler to work on this street after the childhood she endured. He reached Mass Avenue and began to cross the long flat bridge across the Charles.

The river was choppy today. So were the skylines of Boston and Cambridge. The triangular Zakim Bridge at the focal point downriver united the two cities. He stopped in the middle of the long flat bridge and called Ted Conover.

*

Dexter Hutchins was incarcerated on the top floor of the soon-to-be closed court house. Hutchins was a broad-shouldered man with wild hair. He entered the visitors room half-heartedly and sat sidesaddle, as if poised to make a quick getaway.

"My name is Jim Randall. I'm a retired Massachusetts judge. I was on a panel at the Divinity School with Melvin Watson the night he died."

Hutchins squinted. "So?"

"I'm following up on the murder on my own, and I have a few questions. Ted Conover, the DA, gave me the okay to talk to you."

"Shouldn't my lawyer be here?"

"Why do you need a lawyer, you already made a confession. But I believe you may not know the whole story. I believe you may have confessed to more than you're responsible for. If I'm right, it's to your advantage to talk to me because I'm the only one still pursuing the matter."

Hutchins straightened his shoulders. "I'm a very smart man. Everybody treats me as if I'm stupid because I live on the streets. Smart people fall on hard times too, you know."

"I do. And Ted told me that you once were an eminent brain researcher. He said there are questions about your mental stability but not about your intelligence."

"Good, you understand. I'll talk to you, but if I think you're trying to trick me, I'll want my lawyer. What do you want to know?"

"You admitted to hitting Watson with a pipe but were hazy on the details, is that correct?"

"My fingerprints were on the pipe, so I must have hit him."

"You don't remember hitting him?"

"I remember fighting with him, pushing and shoving, and so forth. He treated me like filth. I had had enough."

"You left him lying on the ground. Was he conscious?"

"I don't know. I knew I'd be in trouble if I got caught – who would believe me? So I ran."

"This is important. He died from injuries to the brain caused by repeated blows. Whoever killed him hit him again and again. Do you have any recollection of doing that?"

Hutchins thought carefully. "Sorry. Everything's hazy."

"Ted told me the attorney appointed to represent you is one of the good ones. Are you satisfied with him?"

"He seems fine to me. Earnest but overworked."

"A word of advice from a former judge. Be very careful what you admit to. Don't let anybody persuade you to say anything you are uncomfortable with."

Hutchins leaned back to regard Jim. "I like you. Are you married?"

"I was. My wife died years ago."

"I was married, loved my wife. I took to drink to quiet the voices in my head, at least that's the excuse I gave myself. And Sheila left me. Can't blame her. I never hit her, but I was useless. My research tanked. The bottom of the barrel is a lot closer than people think, and when you hit bottom there's comfort in knowing you can't sink any lower. I don't know why I'm telling you this except that I think you'll understand."

"I do, I saw a lot of hard cases in court. Which do you miss more, your research or your wife?"

"Holy Mother of God, what a question! I know I'm supposed to say my wife but in truth, I think it's my research. I was closing in on the secrets of the brain."

"Did that scare you?"

"It did! I felt god-like, and I'm not qualified to be God. Judge, am I going to die?"

"There's no death penalty in Massachusetts."

"But the FBI was investigating, and there is a federal death penalty."

"The FBI has turned the case over to the state. You don't face the death penalty."

"Why hasn't my attorney told me that?"

"He's undoubtedly swamped. Public defenders have heavy caseloads. I'm sure he'll tell you the next time he sees you."

Hutchins nodded and got to his feet. "Time to go. Good talking to you. I don't get many visitors."

"If I speak to your ex-wife, will you be okay with that?"

Still on his feet Hutchins said, "Sheila? Why should I mind? She'll tell you the same thing I did."

"Does she live in the area?"

"Danvers. On Elm Street."

Jim remembered a lawsuit alleging corruption by a Danvers councilman. The suit chewed up weeks of court time but ultimately Jim threw the case out. He expected applause when he crossed the town border.

Danvers was a mixture of quaint and commercial. He found Elm Street without any trouble. Sheila Hutchins lived in a condo carved out of a former brick schoolhouse. She was expecting him.

"Thanks for agreeing to see me," Jim said.

"How did Dexter seem?" Sheila asked.

"Lucid. Chastened. When did you last see him?"

"Two, three years ago. Is he guilty?"

"I don't know. He admits to some sort of altercation with Melvin Watson but isn't sure what happened. What I wanted to ask is if you can tell me anything about him that will help me understand what may have happened the night of the murder."

Sheila Hutchins shook her head. She was a woman of regal bearing and threadbare clothes. "Is Dexter a violent man? No, that's what's so shocking to me. To even get in a fight is so unlike him, at least when I knew him. Granted, drink can change a man."

"He is obviously intelligent. Even if I didn't know his credentials, I'd sense that from talking to him."

"Brilliant. Mercurial but brilliant."

"Mercurial how?"

"In mood. He could swing from high to low very quickly."

"Hot tempered?"

"Never. If anything too passive. Melvin Watson must have deeply insulted him for Dex to react the way he did."

"I can personally vouch for the fact that Watson was a deeply insulting man. He physically assaulted me the night he died, and unlike your ex-husband, I have a temper. If we hadn't been in front an auditorium full of people, who knows what might have happened."

Sheila Hutchins asked, "Is it possible Dex is confessing to something that didn't happen?"

"Certainly. It happens all the time. Confessions are only slightly more reliable than eyewitness testimony, and eyewitness testimony is notoriously unreliable. Memories can be implanted during interrogations, intentionally or accidentally, and there is a normal human tendency to want to please your interrogator, especially if you are living on the street and have had run-ins with the police. Homeless people lose their dignity quickly, and that makes them susceptible to manipulation."

"It is so sad. I loved him. Still do, but I hate him too."

"For what it's worth, he takes the blame for the divorce. Has nothing bad to say about you."

"That doesn't surprise me."

"He said he never hit you."

"He never did. Hit the bottle, not me."

The more he learned, the less he knew. Jim drove back to Cambridge dispirited. Sheila Hutchins seemed a very nice person, and Dexter Hutchins seemed human underneath layers of shame and brilliance.

9

Ted Conover's office always struck Jim as utilitarian, but this morning it seemed especially so. Jim didn't know why because he couldn't see any physical changes. Something about the mood, perhaps.

Ted slumped behind his desk. "Do you have any idea how tired I get of lowlife? If I could be anything other than a human, I might switch."

"We leave something to be desired, that's for sure."

"What did you learn from Dexter Hutchins?"

"That none of us are immune. We all can fall. I spoke to his ex-wife too. Two fundamentally good people. I feel sorry for them."

Ted's voice lost its edge. "Could he tell you any details about his fight with Watson?"

"No, and I don't think he's deliberately withholding anything. I think the man is habitually confused these days. His ex-wife confirms he had no history of violence, was physically passive in fact."

"Sometimes passive people under the influence can violently explode."

"And that can't be ruled out in Hutchins's case, but I still lean to there being a third party."

"Who ranks high on your hit list?" Ted asked.

"Glen Masters had motive, and Rachel Masters may be involved. Maybe Glen Masters had a dual motive – to merge The Greater Glory with The Greater Good, forming, if you will, The Greatest Good, *and* to avenge his wife for some wrong Melvin Watson did her."

"That seems a stretch to me."

"Me too. I'm only speculating. I'm not satisfied with any answer I can come up with."

"Officially we are proceeding as if Dexter Hutchins is the sole culprit."

"Of course."

"But I can quickly change course if new evidence arises."

"I think that's my cue to keep digging."

"Jim, in your unofficial role, you can talk to people in a way we can't. And since you are a former member of the court, I know you have the interests of justice at heart."

*

Time to talk to Sara again. She had said no to him last time, but he thought he could change her mind. She said no this time, too.

"Come on, Sara. Talk to me. I have lots to tell you."

"Like what?"

"Not going to tell you unless we meet. The Long Gone tomorrow?"

Long pause. "All right. What time?"

For the first time in Jim's memory The Long Gone was completely full – every chair, every table taken, not to mention the three stools at the front window.

"Let's go next door," Jim said to Sara who looked tidy and polished.

The Irish bar next door could get noisy in the evening, but in the afternoon there were only two or three people drinking at the bar.

Jim and Sara sat at a table. "What'll you have?"

"A vodka tonic."

Jim raised an eyebrow. "Not what I would have thought."

"What did you think?"

"Coffee or white wine."

A young woman came to the table to take their orders. "Vodka tonic and a Côtes du Rhône, please." To Sara when the young woman had left, "There's live music here Fridays and Saturdays. Fiddles and guitars."

"I don't think of you going out at night," Sara said.

"I usually don't. Pat likes fiddles, so we come occasionally."

Sara set her face. "What do you want to tell me?"

"I spoke to Dexter Hutchins and Hutchins's ex-wife, and to a young woman who escaped The Greater Glory."

Sara looked astonished but her voice didn't change. "You've been busy."

"And what I heard reinforced my feeling that we don't have the whole story. And I ask you again to search your memory for anything you know about Glen Masters or Melvin Watson, anything from the summers your family spent near the compounds, anything from the time you lived with Masters and your mother after your father left. There must be something, some fact, some conversation, that can shed light on subsequent events."

"Why must there be? You're making assumptions."

"Call them hypotheses, from which I hope to deduce the truth."

Their drinks arrived. Sara concentrated on hers for a moment. She tasted it, put it down. "Alright, let's suppose we don't know the full story. What's missing? Just suppose."

"That someone finished the job Dexter Hutchins started."

Sara nodded. "So Hutchins and Watson get into a fight, what happens next?"

"Hutchins knocks Watson unconscious and runs away knowing the police won't believe him – a homeless drunk – if he's caught. Someone sees the fight between Watson and Hutchins, someone with a grudge against Watson, and takes advantage of the opportunity to kill Watson when Hutchins runs away."

Sara said, "But only Hutchins's fingerprints were on the murder weapon."

"We know that Hutchins hit Watson with the pipe, but maybe the blow or blows didn't kill him. Maybe someone else watched the fight and used another heavy object – a rock, for instance – to kill Watson."

"There is no evidence to support any hypotheses other than Hutchins is the killer."

"Glen Masters is actively recruiting members of The Greater Glory for his group, doesn't that suggest motive?"

"Jim, this has been fun, but I believe the official explanation. "

*

Over dinner at Pat's that night, Jim told her what had happened.

"So maybe it was Dexter Hutchins, after all," he said in conclusion. "Sounds that way. What are you going to do now?"

"Go to Vermont."

Pat offered to come, but Jim demurred. "I need to brood. Best done alone."

He picked up cold cuts at the convenience store in town, then drove to his house on the ridge. It was mid-afternoon and the sun was bright. He entered his house, stuck the cold cuts in the refrigerator, then stood by the long windows. The valley was lost in the glare of the sun. It would emerge at dusk, he knew. He would time dinner to catch the spectacle.

He texted Pat. "I'm here."

"Solve the crime yet?" she texted back.

"You're cruel."

"I miss you already."

"Stop it. You'll make an old man horny."

"That would be a first."

He put away his phone and brooded. The trouble with brooding is it never led anywhere if done consciously. He had to put the crime out of his mind and let thoughts drift into his head unbidden.

He sat at the living room table with a glass of Fitou and thought of everything but the crime. The Red Sox, the price of gas, his thinning hair. He needed stronger reading glasses – maybe even bifocals. He had liked being a judge. Would he repeat his life if he could? You bet, with caveats – less grumbling, more openness. Pat. Joyce.

Children? Maybe he would have been a good father, maybe not. Joyce had been devastated they couldn't have children. Pat didn't seem to mind she never had any. Hard to read another's mind, which never stopped him from trying.

He was good and drunk by dinnertime, which made the valley light almost psychedelic. Bands of pink like stripes on a flag, the river seeming to hover above the riverbed.

In the morning, he made himself a cup of coffee, then drove across New Hampshire to The Greater Good, arriving before noon. Glen Masters was not at home.

"He went across the border," Rachel Masters told him.

Did he need a passport? Jim wanted to ask. "May I talk to you?" he did ask.

Warily, she let him inside. "I don't know why you want to talk to me," she said, leading him to the living room table. "I've told you everything I know."

"What was Sara like as a youngster?"

"Very different."

"How so?"

Rachel Masters seemed uncomfortable but continued talking. "Sara was a wonderful girl. Endless curiosity and kindness, a real sweetheart. Everybody who saw her fell in love. I know that's hard to believe now that she has closed herself off."

"Any idea why she did?"

"Sara was very upset when I left her father. She never forgave me. She was very close to her father."

"How did she feel about Glen?"

Rachel eyes grew distant. "That's what I've never understood. She liked Glen but couldn't understand why I did. It baffled me. Still does."

"Did she have friends growing up?"

"Of course. She was a normal girl in every way. She did well in school, made friends easily."

"Did she have friends in the two compounds when you summered near here?"

Rachel nodded. "The only young people near us in the summer were from The Greater Good and The Greater Glory, so yes, she made friends here."

"The religious nature of the communities didn't bother her?"

"Not at first, only when she became a teenager."

"Could that be why she resents you?"

"I don't understand."

"Could she blame religion for ending your marriage?"

"I've wondered about that."

The front door opened and Glen Masters walked in. He looked unhappy to see Jim. "I thought I recognized your car. What do you want this time?"

Jim was taken aback. Masters, who had seemed like a nice guy before, seemed frightening this time. "I had a few more questions for your wife."

"You've bothered her enough."

"Perhaps you should check with her. The questions I asked were about Sara, and she didn't seem to mind sharing memories." Jim looked at Rachel. "Did I read you correctly?"

Rachel nodded but seemed afraid.

Glen Masters came and stood by the table. "I humored you, Randall, but I've had enough. We had nothing to do with Melvin's death. Leave us alone."

"Your wife told me that you were visiting The Greater Glory again. Are you going to merge the two Greaters?"

Masters took a step closer. "None of your business. I want you to leave now."

Jim rose to his feet as slowly as he could and faced Masters. "I'll leave, but you should be careful about appearances. Watson's only been dead a short time and you're already taking advantage. Doesn't look good."

Masters growled and reached for Jim's shirt. "I'll show you…"

Jim had been surprised when Watson grabbed him the night of the panel but was ready for Masters.

He grasped Masters's wrist. Masters was the stronger, but Jim had surprising strength. "I'll go, but you are digging yourself in deeper. As a former judge, I have seen a lot of guilty men, and you are behaving like one."

"Get out." Unmistakable menace.

Jim went to the door. "One last question. Did you do something that turned Sara against her mother?"

With a guttural roar, Masters charged him, but Jim was out the door.

10

Jim's breathing didn't settle down until he was halfway home. Well, that didn't go as expected, he said to himself. Why can't you leave well enough alone?

Somewhere on the drive home he had the thought that his problem wasn't insatiable curiosity, it was a refusal to accept the dangers of curiosity.

He called Pat when he reached Cambridge. "I'm home."

"Welcome back. How are you?"

"I haven't been gone that long. How different could I be?"

"Very."

"I dodged the usual physical danger, you know how my life is these days."

"Wait, you're serious."

"Glen Masters flew off the handle. Don't worry, I beat the crap out of him."

The usual banter disappeared from Pat's voice. "You *must* take care of yourself. I mean it."

"Thank you. I agree and will try harder."

He climbed to his study and sank into his leather chair. He had seen a side of Masters he hadn't before, and it changed the equation. Motive plus temper equaled a likely killer.

He met with Sara again. On her turf.

"I visited your mother again," he said in her office.

Sara took the news better this time. "How did she seem?"

"She seemed fine, but Glen Masters displayed a temper I hadn't seen."

"I could have told you."

"Why didn't you?"

"Haven't you noticed my reluctance to say much about him?"

"I have, and I asked your mother about it. She said you changed when she left your father."

Sara shook her head in dismay. "She just doesn't get it. I hate anything that gets in the way of thought. Glen's religion precludes thought, and he brainwashed my mother."

"So it wasn't the divorce that estranged you?"

"When my mother split from Dad, it made me very, very sad, but divorce happens. What I couldn't and can't abide is Glen's war on thought. I believe in the brain. I believe in the power of thinking."

Sara's office was stark to begin with, but her words took the air out of the room. Jim shifted in his chair. "I don't get you, Sara. You are pure thought yet when we discuss your mother or Glen, fury shows through your words. What gives?"

"And I don't get you, Jim. You were a judge yet you question me like a shrink."

"I guess we have a lot to learn about each other. Join me and Pat for dinner at our favorite place. We can discover more things we don't understand about each other."

"If you promise to lay off the shrink stuff."

*

Duck, Duck, Goose was fully booked when Jim called to make a reservation, but Bruce said he'd fit the three of them in.

"Two crusty ex-judges and a philosopher," Jim said after they were seated. "Should be a lively evening."

Pat said to Sara, "Ignore him."

Sara seemed, for her, lighthearted. "Hard to do."

"Yes, it is. But it's worth it. Underneath the know-it-all, he's actually a kind man."

Jim puffed himself up. "I don't know it all, but I know everything that matters."

Pat spoke to Sara. "Wait until he has some wine in him. It gets worse."

"Red or white?"

"Red, always red."

Sara, it turned out, was a gourmand, eating with a gusto which precluded most conversation. She wasn't above using her hands. As she dug in, Jim exchanged glances with Pat. Finally, Jim couldn't help himself. "Food deprived as a child?" he asked Sara.

Sara lowered the rib she was gnawing. "We weren't going to talk about families."

"I'm not, I'm talking about food."

Sara wiped her hands and mouth. "I like food, very much."

"I can see."

"Don't you?"

"Not really."

Pat jumped in. "He can't cook. At all. I'm curious, what made you decide on philosophy?"

"Partly as a reaction to my mother and stepfather's rigid religion, I suppose, but honestly, I have no idea except that I like things of the mind, the more rigorous the better. I like the mental challenge of thinking about fundamental questions."

"Theologians think about fundamental questions, too."

"Yes, but they have an easy answer when they come up empty: God."

"Do you like the teaching part of your work?"

"I do. Teaching keeps me fresh. My students inspire me. But if I could do anything I wanted, with no consideration of how to support myself, I'd be a desert mystic."

Jim laughed. "I can see it."

Pat pressed a finger to her temple. "I can picture Jim alone in the desert. He'd be very happy except he'd have no one to complain to."

Jim rolled his eyes. "I wasn't treated this way when I was on the bench."

Sara's eyes brightened. "I never have dessert. I'm going to have dessert."

They lingered over coffee. Sara didn't seem in a hurry to go home. Jim wondered why, given that she had resented him earlier when he asked about her mother. He had the feeling – not for the first time – that if he could figure her out, he would understand the circumstances of Watson's murder, if not who done it.

"Do you want us to walk you home?" Jim asked outside the restaurant.

"No, it's safe."

"Except when someone gets murdered."

"Watson's death was an outlier."

"Did you see or hear anything out of the ordinary when you walked home that night?"

"You asked me before."

"Tell me again."

"Watson's body was found behind the school. I walked in front."

"That's a quiet neighborhood. Sounds carry at night."

"I heard nothing." Sara, annoyed, shook her head. "I'm tired, I'd better get home before I fall asleep."

They parted outside the restaurant. "Thanks for suggesting this," Sara said. "Great food."

Pat said, "I'm glad we had a chance to talk."

Sara smiled. "Me too."

Jim and Pat walked the short distance home. "What do you think?" Jim asked.

"I know you are challenged by enigmas, but she is sending us clear signals. She likes us, especially you, but wants to keep us at arm's length."

"But why?"

"That's her personality, Jim."

"Is that the only reason?"

"Do you think she knows more about the murder than she's telling you?"

"Maybe, but maybe what I sense has nothing to do with murder and everything to do with her mother and Glen and her childhood."

They reached Jim's house. Jim unlocked his door.

"That's what I intend to find out," he said, reaching for the light switch.

*

He called Sasha Cohen at the *Boston Globe*. Jim liked Sasha's eagerness, her zest. He hoped that reporting for a big daily like the *Boston Globe* instead of an alternative weekly wouldn't erode her enthusiasm. "Hi, Sasha. It's Jim Randall."

"Hi, Jim. Are you calling about the Watson murder? We don't have anyone covering that now. Our editors are satisfied the police have the right man."

"You're right, that's why I'm calling."

"Knowing you, I assume that means you retain doubts about Dexter Hutchins's guilt."

"I do, and I can't give you good reasons. Just a hunch."

"I assume you know that a trial date has been set."

"No, I didn't know."

"Two months from now. They're fast-tracking this one."

Jim called Ted as soon as he got off the phone with Sasha. "I hear you've set a trial date for Dexter Hutchins."

"Yes. We have more than enough evidence to go to trial."

"Are you satisfied with what you've got?"

"I'm rarely satisfied. There's always more to know. But we have to go to trial when we believe we have enough evidence. That's our job."

"I don't fault you, Ted, you know that. But one of the advantages of being outside the court system is that I have more leeway than you do."

"Which can be valuable to me. Let me know what you find. Trial dates can be changed."

Jim was alone in his house. Pat was teaching an evening course on the law at the Cambridge Center for Adult Education. She seemed happy, but it meant Jim was alone for longer periods than when she was home writing. That was okay; he liked seeing her happy, especially since he had been worried how she'd fare once she finished the memoir.

He took himself to The Long Gone, needing solitude amidst company. As he walked he asked himself, What piece of the puzzle am I missing? Who do I need to talk to?

The small windows of The Long Gone shielded Jim from the bright light outdoors. Dim light for minor revelations. He sat and thought, the only patron who wasn't staring at an electronic device. He needed an app to find the killer. A killer app. Talk to Ernie. Get a laugh. No, Ernie wouldn't laugh; he'd get the joke but wouldn't laugh.

He liked Ernie; didn't at first, now wondered why everyone couldn't be earnest like Ernie. You're doing it again, Randall: diverting yourself with pleasant thoughts instead of getting to the point. Stop it.

Jim scrolled though a mental list of those he had talked to about Watson's murder, and those he hadn't. Sara's father stood out among the latter. Hutchins, Sara, Glen and Rachel Masters – yes, yes, and yes. Sara's father – not yet.

He checked his watch when he left the coffee shop an hour later. Time flies when you are sorting clues.

He walked with purpose past the live poultry shop, always a talisman, and Beauty Shop Row before he reached the MIT campus, interwoven with the city. Sara was teaching a class. He snuck in the rear of the lecture hall and watched.

Sara paced ceaselessly behind the lectern, rarely glancing at her audience. Her hands were more animated than he had ever seen, darting this way and that.

How fascinating: this shut tight woman sculpturing thought with her hands.

Before the end of the hour she spotted Jim and paused for a moment. Those in class who were paying attention looked to see whom their professor was gawking at.

The class ended. Sara gathered her papers and approached the back of the room. "What did you think of my lecture?"

"You are definitely into your subject. Can we go somewhere and talk?"

There was a coffee alcove off the Infinite Corridor and some sofas to sit on. High-ceilinged windows framed the sitting area. Sara perched the coffee cup on her knees. "I always wonder, am I reaching my students?"

"You reached me."

"Really? You got caught up in what I was saying?"

"Certainly, and you did too. I like someone who's enthralled by their subject."

"I'm flattered. What did you want to ask me?"

"I'd like to talk to your father."

Sara shook her head emphatically. "I wondered why you were here. You hoped to catch me with my guard down. I told you no. I meant it."

"I know you did, but until I talk to your father, I don't have the complete picture."

"Of what? The murder?"

"Of Watson's cult."

"I won't let you talk to him. Not in a million years. He has been hurt enough. He's happy now, and that's the way he shall remain."

"It would upset him to talk about The Greater Glory? After so much time?"

"You don't know my dad. He's a sensitive man and still can't understand why my mother left him for a fanatic."

"I want to talk to him about Watson."

"Dad simply can't fathom people who squander thought for dogma, and Watson is worse than Masters. It is painful to watch Dad struggle to understand. I won't let you put him through that."

"Sara, I'm sorry to upset you. I'll drop the subject for now. If you change your mind, let me know. I understand how sensitive this is for you and your family, and I promise I will tread extra carefully if I get the chance to talk to him."

"Which you won't. Ever," Sara said. Jim watched her walk away.

The Infinite Corridor runs the length of MIT's spine. Twice a year the sun shines the entire length of the corridor, from one end to the other, which at MIT becomes an occasion of calculation and wonder. In very early times, such natural phenomena would have led to human sacrifice. Present day geeks faced with unexplained phenomena don't sacrifice, they do math.

Jim watched Sara stride the corridor. A hyper-rationalist striding an infinite corridor of math and science through a world gone crazy. He felt sorry for her. Sorry for her personal struggle, sorry to put her through remembering.

11

In his study, reading after dinner. Pat downstairs, reviewing notes for her class. Equilibrium except for Dexter Hutchins's unconvincing confession. Why couldn't Jim accept his confession as the final word?

As a judge, he would have. Or would he? He thought back: on the bench he would have processed the confession differently, reviewed it logically, scrutinized it for consistency. By contrast – and exaggerating slightly – now he was winging it.

Improvising instead of reading sheet music. Trusting his gut to know more than his mind, or at least reach into crevices his logical mind couldn't. Instinct is part of our brains, why not use it? Based on his post-judicial experiences, he would say that instinct fits the pieces of the puzzle together. He didn't mean emotion; emotion could lead one astray. Instinct. Intuition. Gut. That's what he was talking about.

His gut told him that Hutchins didn't do it. Jim put down the Cicero he was reading ("In Defense of Gaius Rabirius") and reviewed why he reached that conclusion.

Watson was an intentionally inflammatory man. To the insecure, inflammatory rhetoric promised certainty. To the lost in need of a leader, inflammatory rhetoric spelled, "follow me." Watson's inflammatory rhetoric had attracted followers but also triggered extreme hatred. That such a hated man could meet his death at the hands of a hapless drunk he happened upon behind the Divinity School seemed too far-fetched to believe. Jim didn't.

He got up from his chair, legs stiff from sitting, and went downstairs. He found Pat in the kitchen, raiding the refrigerator. "I thought you never snacked."

"Only when you're not watching."

"I'm going up to Maine again, and this time I'm going to nose around until I find something."

"Be careful, Jim. You may push whoever killed Watson over the edge."

"I'll take that chance."

*

He left on a clear day. The seasons were changing, or more accurately were about to change: hints of change in the air. Lower humidity crystallized vision. When he briefly drove along the coast, the ocean had acquired density, looked solid, as if it had turned into metal. Then the road curved inland and he lost sight of the water.

He stopped when he came to the lake where Sara Vincent and her parents had summered. The lake was not a tourist destination; too small, the shore too crowded with summer homes. There was a motel on the road north of the lake, and that's where Jim asked for a room, regretting his choice as soon as he saw the room.

The motel was pre-Holiday Inn, an elongated shack with an empty parking lot and a near-extinction neon sign. No cockroaches, at least that he could see in a quick visual inspection of the room. At least there was that, but if the sink had ever been cleaned, he couldn't tell.

He turned down the bed. Clean sheets at least. An "at least" room. It would do. To absorb the atmosphere of an area, one should avoid anodyne (or sanitized) rooms.

He sat on the bed and called Pat. "I'm at a motel."

"Dare I ask the name?"

"The Easy Comfort Motel. Don't probe. That's all I'm going to say."

"What's your plan of action?"

"No plan. Keep my mind out of this. See what I can see. Use my sixth sense."

"If this works, it will revolutionize crime solving."

"I'll call you after I solve the crime, or tomorrow, whichever comes first."

The mattress was comfortable, it turned out, and he slept soundly, undisturbed by dreams. He awoke to a sparkling morning and ate at the nearby diner. The eggs were good, the toast came with raspberry jam, not the usual grape, and the coffee was hot but not scalding. Not a bad start to a day that promised to be difficult.

He wandered to the lake and got out of the car. He couldn't stand at the water's edge because of the summer houses, but he was close enough to imagine living by the lake. Dish antennas on some roofs. Short docks and small boats. Little to no space between houses – he hoped the owners liked each other. He tried to imagine Sara and her parents summering in one of these houses, close enough to the compounds to walk, not close enough to be caught up in their business. He tried to imagine what Sara had been like as a child, as a teen.

She had been open to the world then, her mother had said. Had Sara's face reflected that? Did she have more than one expression? Once again, Jim had circled back to the nagging question: What could have closed Sara down? Both Sara and her mother agreed that the remarriage played a part – Sara said she couldn't abide her mother's fundamentalism, her mother said that Sara couldn't forgive her for divorcing Sara's father.

Jim strolled the road by the lake, head down, not looking, not seeing, exploring the inner terrain of his imagination. Imagination and memory merged, and he remembered Watson grabbing his shirt at the Divinity School, pissing Jim off even though he knew Watson was posturing for YouTube. Had Watson done the equivalent to Glen Masters to drive him away, to cause him to start his own compound, some sort of goading or threat? Or could the reason have been the romantic triangle with Watson, Masters, and Sara's mother?

Hard to imagine but not impossible. Rachel Masters seemed to Jim a sexless woman, but who knows what she was like then? Or maybe the love triangle – if there ever was one – was mainly a fight for power between Watson and Masters, with Rachel the prize but not a player.

He came to a barrier in the road. "No Trespassing," read the sign. Beyond was The Greater Glory, and beyond that, The Greater Good. He walked around the barrier and entered the compound. He heard a dog barking. No sign of people, the same as last time. He stopped in the middle of the compound and waited.

Long minutes passed. Finally, a stalwart woman emerged from a house and approached. "You're trespassing," she said.

"Remember me? I was with Glen Masters the last time I came. Is he here now?"

"No. Who are you?"

"Judge Randall, formerly of the Massachusetts Superior Court. Have you lived here long?"

"None of your business."

"Did you know Sara Vincent?"

That stopped the woman cold. She fumbled for words. "Sara? Do you know her?"

"Yes. Were you here when Sara and her parents summered nearby?"

The woman nodded. "How is she? I worried about her."

"Why?"

"She was sweet. We were friends."

"So you knew each other when you were children."

"Teens. Then I never saw her again. Is she okay?"

"Yes. She's a professor at MIT."

"No kidding? The Lord works in wondrous ways. How is her daughter?"

"What daughter?"

The woman looked stricken. "I shouldn't have said anything. I thought you knew!" She hurried towards her house. "Don't tell Sara I told you!" she called over her shoulder as she slammed the door behind her.

What the hell was the woman talking about? Sara had never mentioned a daughter. Jim stood in the middle of the compound, trying to absorb this information.

An angry voice came from behind him. "Randall! I told you not to come here."

Jim turned. Masters, who looked ready to kill.

"What are you doing here?" Masters yelled, advancing.

"Finding out what I can." Stay calm, Randall. He couldn't be angrier than Masters, given how angry he was, so out-calm him. "Good to see you. How are you?"

"Don't be cute. How did you get in here?"

"On foot."

"Didn't you see the no trespassing sign?"

"I did, and I ignored it."

"Get out. Go. And stay away. I don't want to see you again. And neither does Rachel."

"Why didn't either of you tell me Sara has a daughter?"

Masters glared. "Get out! Get out before I throw you out!"

"I'll go. But I guarantee you, whatever you're hiding will come out one day. You may feel insular in your little world, but your compound has no walls."

"That's it." Master advanced a step. "Get out!"

Jim turned to go. "How does your god feel about your cult? Does he applaud? I think he cries. By the way, what's your granddaughter's name?"

Jim hurried away, leaving the same way he came in. Once he passed the no trespassing sign, he realized his heart was pounding.

Jim retraced his steps to his car. He needed to think hard. He drove slowly through back roads, his mind going faster than his car.

Sara has a daughter. What does that mean? She apparently had her daughter when she was a teenager, which meant the daughter must still be young. Where was she? Not with Sara, at least as far as he knew.

He thought of calling Sara from the road, but thought better of it. Better to talk in person. He predicted she'd be defensive, evasive; he wondered if her face would reveal things she wouldn't.

The drive seemed very long, bordering on endless. He arrived home exhausted. He didn't bother to go up to his study, he collapsed in his chair in the living room and breathed deeply.

He called Pat when he got his wind back. "An unusually eventful trip," he began. "I got chased out of The Greater Glory by Glen Masters and learned that Sara Vincent has a daughter."

Very little caught Pat off-guard, but this did. She slowly repeated Jim's words to make sure she had heard them. "Sara Vincent has a daughter."

"Yes."

"How old is the daughter? Where is she?"

"I don't know anything more than I told you. And I only learned this from a woman in the compound, who looked stricken when she realized I hadn't known. Then Glen Masters showed up, not happy that I was there and even more unhappy when I asked about Sara's daughter. Yours truly would have been beaten to a pulp if I had hung around."

"Oh, Jim, this is not good."

"Well, I've gone too far to turn back. Help me plan this. What's the best way to ask Sara about her daughter?"

Duck, Duck, Goose. The three of them. No heads up to Sara about the reason, although Jim casually mentioned that he had visited The Greater Glory again.

Sara looked tailored. Her hair was up, her clothes had shape and cut. Jim almost thought she had been tipped off about his purpose and had spruced up her appearance to throw him off guard. But that was impossible.

Bruce had seated them at Jim and Pat's usual table near the window.

Jim started the conversation. "Before you ask, I went up to Maine without a plan and after a night's rest, found myself walking along the shore road of the lake where you summered when you were a child."

"A teen. We started going there when I was twelve," Sara corrected.

"Okay. And I came to the entrance to The Greater Glory. There was a no trespassing sign which I ignored and walked in." Jim paused. He liked Sara, was sorry he had to upset her. "There I talked to a woman, she didn't tell me her name, and in the course of our conversation, she asked about your daughter." Jim stopped because he had rarely seen a look of anguish like the one that appeared on Sara's composed face. It almost made Jim gasp. "Don't," he reached for her shoulder.

Sara went through the seven stages of grief in front of his eyes. She buried her face in her hands, raised her head, sniffled back tears, and finally reached out in desperation for Pat's hand.

If there were other sounds in the restaurant, Jim didn't hear; all he heard was Sara's breathing, her sighs.

"I'm sorry, I had to ask," he said.

Sara sniffled one last time. "I gave Ruth up as soon as she was born. And that's all I'm going to say about her."

"Where is she now?"

"Don't ask me. I will walk out and I'll make a scene."

Jim and Pat exchanged glances. "Of course," Pat acknowledged. "We'll respect your feelings. It must have been hard for you."

"You have no idea."

Jim spoke quietly. "For what it's worth, the woman seemed concerned for your daughter's well-being."

"Was the woman's name Naomi?"

"She didn't tell me her name. I was standing in the middle of the compound talking to her when Glen Masters appeared. I hadn't seen his angry, threatening side before. It wasn't pretty."

"Glen is the nicest man in the world, until he isn't," Sara said. She stopped. "This is all my fault, isn't it?"

"No, Sara, none of it is your fault."

Sara raised her menu. "I won't talk about Ruth, not now, not ever. I'm hungry. What do you recommend?"

Dinner was up to Duck, Duck, Goose's standards, and no one watching could have guessed that Jim, Pat, and Sara were skirting an incendiary topic the entire meal; anyone watching would have sworn they were having a relaxed good time.

On the sidewalk outside the restaurant. "One question, and then we'll let you go," Jim said. "How old were you when Ruth was born?"

"I said no more questions."

"Only one."

"I was fifteen. I'll say goodnight now."

"Goodnight, Sara," Pat said.

Jim and Pat were silent at first, but as they turned the corner to Jim's townhouse, Jim said, "Well, that explains why Sara closed down."

He could sense what Pat was going to say before she said it. "Not entirely. I'm sure there's more," Pat said as they reached his townhouse. "And she'll never tell us what it is, I'm sure of that too."

12

"Dexter Hutchins wants to see you." It was Ted Conover on the phone, catching Jim off-guard.

"Any idea why?"

"None. All his attorney would tell me is that Hutchins trusts you."

"And his attorney is okay with this?"

"Yes. What do you say?"

"Sure. I moonlight as a priest. I listen to confessions."

"Don't get your hopes up, Father. My guess is he wants to complain about his cell."

"I'll bring my robes and my vestments, just in case."

The visitors room at the Middlesex Jail was only a few floors above Jim's old courtroom, which gave Jim pause. Hutchins was clean-shaven and his hair had been cut, rendering him almost unrecognizable. Except for his prison garb, he looked like the geek he had been, earnest, searching, opaque, not the drunk he became.

"Thanks, Judge. I didn't know if you'd come."

Jim pulled his chair closer to the bench. "Why did you want to see me?"

"I've remembered more about that night, what happened after Watson called me a sinner."

"Go on."

"I hit him, I did, but I didn't hit him hard enough to kill him. My attorney says the autopsy showed repeated blows to the head. That wasn't me. Watson went down quickly and I ran."

"An objective observer might say you are tailoring your memory to fit facts you've learned since your arrest."

Hutchins nodded. "It's possible. I haven't forgotten what I know about the brain. Memory is an amalgamation of impressions from different quadrants of the brain, and how the impressions get assembled into a mental picture can change over time. I get that. But I also know that my original confession was given when my mind was fogged by drink and fear. I'm sober now and on my meds, and my memory is much clearer."

Jim thought for a moment. "What do you want me to do with this information?"

"The first thing I wanted was to see if you believed me. I have lived in a fog for so long, I no longer know if I sound lucid."

"You sound lucid."

"The second reason I wanted to see you is because you seem determined to find the killer and aren't sure it's me."

"Which is true."

"Good, but I don't think the district attorney agrees, and until you find the killer, I'm on the hook."

"No promises," Jim said, before leaving. "I can't pull a murderer out of a hat." Jim took the down elevator but before reaching the lobby, changed his mind and punched the button for the courtroom floor. He hadn't been back in his courtroom since he retired. He peeked in. The courtroom was empty. He stepped inside.

Immediately the smell hurtled him back in time. He never had been able to identify the smell, thought it might have something to do with the flags bracketing the bench, or the accumulated odor of fear. Or maybe the smell was a figment of his imagination – an olfactory version of an imaginary impression.

For a moment, he had an urge to be back on the bench. But then he reflected that freelancing gave him latitude he didn't have as a judge. At times, he felt like a kid out of school. At other times, he wondered what the hell he had gotten himself into.

He left the courtroom, and as he did, almost bumped into a guard he knew. "What were you doing in there?" the guard demanded. "Oh, it's you, Judge Randall. I didn't recognize you. Checking out your old digs?"

Jim faintly smiled. "How are you, Frank?"

"I'm good, real good. How about you?"

"Doing well, thanks. How's the family?"

"My daughter's a freshman at Bowdoin, can you believe it, Judge?"

"That's wonderful, Frank. Good for her." Jim man-slapped Frank's shoulder. "Hope she turns out better than her old man."

Frank chuckled. "I miss you too, Judge."

Jim left the courthouse and caught the number 69 bus home. The tug of the past was strong, but the present wasn't all that bad. After a glass of Cabernet Franc, he called Ted Conover. "Hutchins remembers more and is sure his blow didn't kill Watson. He's counting on me to find the killer. He's given up on you guys."

"Jim, you know as well as I do that murderers often deny guilt after they confess."

"Of course, and Hutchins may be your guy, but my doubts mirror his. I can't see him hitting Watson until he was dead. Lashing out, I can see. One or two blows, yes. There was sustained anger behind the fatal blows."

"A trial date hasn't been set, and I'll delay asking the court for one, but I can't stall indefinitely. If you don't turn up new evidence soon, I'll have to proceed."

"Thanks, Ted."

Jim spent that night at Pat's. Sex was the solution. To the crime, not his private life. He floated the idea with Pat. "I've been searching for a solution in the feud between Watson and Masters, a theological dispute, a battle for followers, but more and more I think the answer lies in sex. If Watson treated his compound as his sexual playground, he was bound to stir up anger. Sex is more primal than power. Power is sought to get sex, not the other way around. In other words, I think the motive for this crime lies deep in human nature. I don't know how Sara's revelation fits into this, but I'm sure it does."

Pat considered her answer. "That sounds about right."

"And maybe someone who escaped The Greater Glory can shed more light on the sexual atmosphere in the compound."

*

Angela Butler resisted at first.

"I'll come to your shop. We can talk on your lunch hour," Jim coaxed.

"Talking about The Greater Glory makes me very uncomfortable."

"Please. A man who may be innocent is in jail."

He hadn't been to Newbury Street since the last time he and Angela talked. How many women's clothing stores could fit on one street, he wondered again? The shop where Angela worked was empty except for her.

"We can talk here," she said. "I can't leave the store. My co-worker called in sick."

Jim knew nothing about men's clothes, and less about women's, but the dresses, jackets, blouses, and skirts hanging on the front racks looked museum-quality. In half of one rack in the back, sportier looking clothes, brighter colors, patterns. No doubt, the sight of him in his "I hate to shop clothes" would drive potential customers away – to them he must look like Dexter Hutchins.

There was a small desk in the rear. They sat there. "What did you want to know?"

"I'd like to get a better idea of life in the compound when you were there. Was there an atmosphere of freedom? Of fear?"

Angela seemed uncomfortable. "Why are you so interested?"

"I want to find out who killed Melvin Watson. I'm in touch with the district attorney and the accused, Dexter Hutchins, but I'm doing this unofficially. You can't get in trouble for anything you tell me, and I promise I will protect your privacy. But I'm not asking for details of what happened to you, I'm interested in life in the compound. What it was like."

"Children are children. I thought our life was normal until I was twelve or thirteen. That's when I realized how perverted life in the compound was, and that's when the fear set in. At first, I talked about it, to my friends, to my mother. But my mother told me not to say anything, and my friends were as frightened as I was."

"Where was your father?"

"I never knew my father. I don't even know who he is. Mom wouldn't tell me."

"Did you leave the compound often?"

"Almost never. We were schooled in the compound, made friends in the compound. Our whole world was the compound."

"There are no fences, just no trespassing signs. You could have left."

"That's what I eventually did. But fear is stronger than any fence. We were repeatedly told that God would keep us out of heaven if we left. Reverend Watson convinced us that he and only he could guide us to heaven. I'm ashamed I ever believed him."

"Did you ever know a girl named Ruth?"

"Ruth was a common name in the compound. What did she look like?"

"I have no idea. I don't even know her last name."

"There was a baby named Ruth who was brought to the compound about the time Watson started sexually abusing me. I don't know where she came from. I know Reverend encouraged his followers to adopt unwanted children. He especially encouraged them to adopt baby girls."

A customer entered the store. Angela excused herself and went to greet her. After a few minutes conversation, she steered the customer to the casual rack and showed her a blouse.

How surreal to be hearing Angela's story of depravity surrounded by clothes few could afford. The customer proved to be choosy and left the store without buying anything. Angela returned to the desk. "What else did you want to ask?" she said.

"You've told me what I wanted to know. You've been helpful."

"I do remember one more thing. Watson held special bible classes for young girls. He taught us that the women of God had a special role, to serve men and to raise children according to God's wishes. He made us proud. I remember how much I liked those classes, three or four of us sitting on the floor around his chair. I felt like one of the chosen. The abuse didn't start until we reached puberty."

As he had last time, Jim walked across the Massachusetts Avenue bridge to Cambridge. He felt sick to his stomach. Watson used piety to disguise depravity. Who could object to the adoption of unwanted children? But what if only girls were adopted? There are monsters among us.

MIT straddled Mass Ave once Jim had crossed the river: the Infinite Corridor to his right, the student center and Kresge Auditorium to his left. He walked the length of the Infinite Corridor to see Sara and emerged on the far end of campus. Sara's office was in a detached building that was slated to be torn down. He lucked out; she was in.

"We have to talk."

"What is it? You look terrible. Sit down. Coffee?"

"No, thanks. Listen, I just spoke to a young woman who grew up in Watson's compound. The world has to learn the full extent of Watson's depravity, it sheds a whole new light on his murder. Whoever killed him will have to be punished, but no judge or jury will be harsh under the circumstances."

Sara didn't move at first. Then she got up and closed her door. "What did the young woman tell you?"

"That Watson indoctrinated young girls, having them sit at his feet, filling them with lies, then sexually abused them when they reached puberty. What made her story especially chilling was to learn that Watson encouraged his followers to adopt unwanted children, to import girls, as it were. Abusing the daughters of followers wasn't enough. Watson was a procurer."

If Jim had expected a visible reaction, he was disappointed. Sara remained stony-faced. She baffled him, how she could be so steely when he expected her to flinch.

She spoke. "What she told you is true, and nothing new. I told you the same thing." Here she paused, a pause so brief as to be forgotten as soon as she resumed speaking, "Except about the adoptions."

"You knew about them?"

Did she flinch then, or was the slight twitch of her eyes a blink? So hard to tell with Sara. "Not really."

"Think, Sara. Did your mother or stepfather say anything about a particularly awful case of abuse, an outraged parent, a scandal in the compound, or anything else that might help us?"

Sara unbent to the extent of leaning forward and spreading her hands. "Jim, you might be wrong to keep looking. The real killer may be Dexter Hutchins."

"Of course, Sara. What kind of an ex-judge do you think I am? I consider all the possibilities."

"Then why don't you relax and let the legal system do its job. That's what you would recommend if you were still a judge."

That hit a nerve. He fumbled for words. Before he could find them, she continued, "Think of the pain you caused the young woman with your questions. Think of the pain it causes me when you question me. You mean well, I know that, but you aren't getting anywhere. Yet you continue to cause pain."

"I take your point."

"Think about it. Let your friend Ted handle the case. Have faith in the system you devoted your life to."

He left the office in a daze, having heard the voice of reason. He couldn't deny anything she said. Kendall Square lay ahead. He needed a dose of the live poultry store and Beauty Shop Row.

Sara's question had shaken him. Had he no faith in the system he had devoted his life to?

He was in such a daze he passed Beauty Shop Row without noticing.

*

Pat came to his house for the night. He could count on her to stabilize him, not only by what she said but by her presence. He didn't breach the topic of Sara's admonition until he had recounted his visit to Angela Butler, and then only tangentially.

"Let's go to Paris, get away from temptation," he said when dinner was finished but before they cleaned up.

"That's a novel reason for going to Paris."

"You said you've been to Paris and loved it. So did I when Joyce and I went."

"You still haven't told me what's going on. What prompted this sudden urge?"

Jim sat back. "I stopped by Sara Vincent's office on my way home from Newbury Street. Something she said shook me up. Maybe I should drop this case, let Ted do his job. He's good, I respect him. I don't know why I feel compelled to muck things up."

"We've talked about this before. Getting to the bottom of things is in your genes. You're doing what comes naturally."

"I wasn't a meddler on the bench."

"Precisely. The inquisitive side of you had to remain dormant. It's got free rein now."

"Free rein but not the right. I'm hurting people."

"Angela Butler?"

"And Sara. Neither wants to talk about Watson or The Greater Glory."

They were drinking Côtes du Rhône. His fallback wine. He took a sip. Pat waited.

"I ask myself why I keep probing, and I always get the same answer. The more I learn about the depravity at The Greater Glory when Watson was alive, the more I'm convinced that Dexter Hutchins assaulted him but that someone else struck the final blows."

Pat nodded. "And as long as you feel that way, you will keep digging, I know you."

"But is it the right thing to do? If I'm hurting people?"

"Ask yourself this. If you prove to be correct, won't you be glad you persisted? Won't it be worth causing temporary pain if it means an innocent person won't be convicted?"

"Yes."

"There's your answer. And yes, I'd love to go to Paris, but after you finish what you started."

"I knew you'd say that."

"You were *hoping* I'd say that. It's the nudge you needed."

"I should have chosen a woman who never wielded a gavel."

"From the myriad women you had to choose from?"

"Exactly. It's decided. We go to Paris after I crack this case."

13

For a week Jim listened to Sara's words, ignored Pat's, for a week he tried forgetting the case, for a week he read in his study, took long walks, and drank more than his usual amount of red wine. By the end of the week he was so grouchy that Pat almost ditched him.

"I told you so," she said.

"Don't be smug."

"Sara's words really got to you, didn't they?"

"She's probably right."

"Since we've been together every attractive young woman you encounter turns your head a little. If Sara were a man, her words wouldn't haunt you the way they did."

"That's not fair. She had a good point."

"Is Ted upset that you're involved?"

"No, doesn't seem so."

"Has Dexter Hutchins's lawyer raised a stink?"

"Again, no."

"I rest my case. I'm curious, if women turn your head as easily as they do, how did you remain faithful to Joyce, and how did you manage without women for so long after she was gone?"

"I'm loyal by nature, and being with you has freed me to look at other women without fear of getting involved."

Pat thought about that for a moment. "I'm still learning about you – I guess I shouldn't be surprised, I kept learning new things about Ralph until the day he died."

"I'm going back to Maine."

"To The Greater Glory?"

"No. To the police station. Want to come?"

"No, thank you."

Jim drove up the next weekend. His mind picked up speed as he drove. Maine was not Vermont, but it was pretty.

He stopped at the police station in town. The officer at the front desk was reluctant at first but after Jim explained who he was and what he wanted, allowed him to look at the police logs. The two Greaters kept problems within their compounds, that was apparent. In recent years, there were only two calls from either compound: one for domestic abuse (the complaint was dropped) and the other for breaking and entering (the thief – a young man from town who had nothing to do with the two Greaters – was caught and convicted).

"Anything that might not have been entered on the logs?"

The desk officer shook his head. "Officially, everything goes in the logs."

"Unofficially?"

The officer shrugged. "Nothing out of the ordinary."

Next stop: the local weekly, a free paper supported by advertising. The editor was flattered by Jim's attention and gladly showed him what they had on the two Greaters, which turned out to be not much. "Controversy is not good for advertising," the editor explained. "We are a feel-good paper."

"What can you tell me off the record?" Jim asked.

"Peace does not prevail between the Greaters. It has always baffled me why one group or the other doesn't go somewhere else. I guess they need a feud."

"Do you anticipate a merger now that Watson is gone?"

"Hard to say. I don't know enough about their inner workings. Does The Greater Glory have a successor-in-waiting? Will the Greaters merge and Glen Masters become the guru of both? Wish I knew."

Before heading home, Jim drove through the countryside absorbing the environs that natured the dueling Greaters. Dense with woods, dotted with lakes, the land refused to stand still. At times it swelled as if it would break out in mountains, and the imagination would soar, but then the land would return to earth. A landscape that stirred the imagination but did not shake it. He wondered: Would a religious sect in the soaring mountains – in contrast to the thick Maine woods – even need a guru?

His opinion of Glen Masters had changed over the course of his visits to Maine. At first Masters had seemed more a withdrawn seeker than a fierce leader, but over time Jim had spied the jagged edges of his persona, the control freak, the man who would have his way no matter what. Jim toyed with the idea of visiting The Greater Good again, but dismissed the idea. He had seen enough of Masters up close and personal. He needed to better understand his context.

Masters hadn't personally killed Watson, Jim still believed, but was he capable of setting the murder in motion? Of that, Jim had no doubt. Jim had witnessed many hard-edged men in court but never a hard-edged man of God. But since being a man of God was a self-anointed position, any fool or scoundrel could become one. Masters was capable of arms-length murder – but did he do it?

What better place to hide one's evil side from the world than in the woods? Freedom Here, Freedom Now, the militia in the Wilcox case, had picked the woods as their weekend hideaway, safe from the blind eyes of the insufficiently paranoid. Woods masked all kinds of frowned-upon behavior.

His train of thought having come to its terminus, he turned and headed home. Three hours later – tired, feeling every one of his sixty-eight years – he reached Pat's apartment and got straight into bed.

"Learn anything?" she asked before he fell completely asleep.

"I'll tell you in the morning."

She started to wash up, but stopped when she heard a plaintive cry, "Pat."

She returned to the bedroom. "What is it? Is something wrong?"

"Thank you for being normal," she thought he said.

"Normal, is that what you said?"

"Yes. Thank you."

She had been leaning down to hear him. "My pleasure." She straightened. "Go to sleep."

In the morning, when he awoke, he was sure he had left something behind in the woods. He got out of bed and checked his wallet and keys. Had both, so it must be something else.

Pat was still asleep. He dressed, then quietly let himself out of the house to clear his lungs. It felt good to walk. He walked downhill, then took a left to the Common, where he tried to think of what he had left in the woods. He realized now it wasn't wallet or keys, it was a piece of the puzzle. A foundational piece. In jigsaw puzzle terms, he had found a corner piece while driving through the Maine countryside but foolishly left it in the woods. Without it, the puzzle would remain incomplete.

A morning drunk wandered the Common in a daze, matted hair a mess. The sun, having surmounted the surrounding buildings, shone in Jim's eyes. He found an empty bench – not difficult at this lonely hour – and concentrated.

Lesson One from the amateur sleuth manual – empty the mind to let the subconscious work, then concentrate like hell. He had done the former in the Maine woods, now he did the latter on a city bench.

He popped up, elated. "Eureka!" he didn't yell but wanted to. Sara's father, that's who he had yet to talk to. Who he had to talk to. Sara's father, who lived in the South End, as close as could be, yet a complete mystery. Sara had said little about him and had refused to let Jim see him, but he had to get her to relent.

He retraced his steps to Pat's apartment, uphill all the way. She was eating breakfast. She didn't seem surprised that he had gone for an early morning walk.

"I need to talk to Sara's father," he announced.

"Okay." Pat's tone was non-committal. She knew her Jim.

"No, I'm serious. He's the corner piece. Until I talk to him I can't complete the puzzle."

"I'm not arguing with you."

"Then why do you sound skeptical?"

"I said okay."

"You didn't sound like you meant it."

She made a megaphone with her hands. "Okay!" She lowered her hands. "Is that better?"

"Much better. Talk like that all the time."

She shooed him away. "Go and let me finish my breakfast."

He waited until mid-morning to call Sara, and when he called, got her voicemail. "Hi, Sara. Jim Randall. Can we meet for coffee? I have something to ask you. You'll say no, but I'll persuade you. I can come to your office or there's always The Long Gone. Let me know. Thanks. Take care."

She didn't return his call until late afternoon. He was rummaging around his townhouse, too restless to read, when she called. "I can meet you at The Long Gone in twenty minutes. And the answer's still no."

"We'll see about that. I'm on my way."

Sara arrived before he did. She had picked a table near the front door, as if poised to make a fast getaway.

"How are you?" He hovered over her before sitting.

Her voice flatlined. "Fine. You want to talk to my father, don't you?"

"Yes. First, coffee." He ordered a dark roast at the counter. When it was poured, he carried it to the table. "Sara, I respect your desire to keep your father out of this, but until I talk to him, I can't solve the puzzle. And I'm determined to do so."

She peered down at her coffee and shook her head in sorrow. "I can't let you. It's not that he's frail," she raised her head, her eyes fierce, "it's that he's ignorant of the mess Mom got herself into. I've kept him in the dark because he takes things to heart and will be stricken if he realizes. And he'll worry himself sick about me. He thinks I'm happy. I won't let you disabuse him."

Jim watched in silence after she finished talking. Her face betrayed nothing. He waited a moment. "I can be diplomatic," he assured her.

"Jim, you are wise, you are blunt, you are fair. Diplomatic is not a word I'd use to describe you."

"Give me more credit. I am sensitive to a man who wanted no part of the Watson-Masters circus."

"Circus. Interesting choice of words. I'm sorry, Jim, I can't let you disturb him. The one noble thing I've done is protect Dad. He's a good soul."

"Will you at least answer a few questions about him?"

"If they don't betray his privacy."

"I seem to remember you telling me you lived with your dad after your parents separated. Do I remember correctly?"

"I briefly lived with my mother and Masters at The Greater Good, then went to live with Dad. Why do you ask?"

"I'm trying to understand him better. And you. You are hard to read, as if you didn't know."

A flicker of acknowledgment. And he understood something more about her, simply from that flicker: she knew herself better than she let on. She wasn't opaque, just cagey. He wondered if the stone face had come easily, or required practice.

He continued. "If I know why you left your mother and went to live with your father, I might understand why you're so protective of him."

"The situation with my mother and Glen Masters had become untenable, that's all you need to know. Dad offered a safe haven for a year before I left for college. I see him on major holidays, but I leave him alone most of the time. It's what he prefers."

"He lives in the South End?"

"Yes. I beg you, do not try to find him. Do not disturb his peace."

"I won't on my own, you have my word, but I'm going to keep pressing in hopes you'll let me." He waited a moment, then, "Are we okay? Are we still allies?"

"Let's say we're not antagonists, how's that?"

Jim, deadpan. "Okay, but if we were allies, I'd treat you to an unforgettable dinner at Duck, Duck, Goose this weekend. But since we're not."

A crooked grin. "What the hell, but only if we talk philosophy, and nothing but philosophy."

"Do I ever talk about anything else?"

Before walking to the restaurant Saturday to meet Sara, Pat checked herself in the bedroom mirror. Around her neck she clasped the simple gold chain that had been a law school graduation gift from her father. She had worn it under her judicial robes, but Jim hadn't known its significance until they became a couple.

"Are you going to be nice to Sara tonight?"

"I'm always nice," Jim answered.

"Lucky you're not under oath."

Bruce seated them near a window. The traffic at the intersection of Beacon and Kirkland was at a standstill – construction.

"Sparkling? Still?" the young waitress chirped.

"Tap is fine," Jim said.

Sara walked in a few minutes later. "Sorry to be late. A math major urgently needed my help." She pulled her chair to the table. "I'm still surprised how some students with quantitative minds struggle with philosophy."

"Why do you stay at MIT?"

"Because if I can open an engineering or science student's mind to philosophy, they will be more likely to consider the context of the work they do after graduation."

"I ordered red wine, is that okay?"

"Red is fine," Sara said.

The waitress approached and held the bottle of wine so that Jim could read the label. "Laguzelle Minervois from the Languedoc." She extracted the cork and poured Jim a taste.

"Very nice," he said and waited until she had poured glasses for the three of them.

Sara continued her thought. "To finish answering your question, Yale offered me a position before I got tenure at MIT, but I like rigorous thinking and MIT students are nothing if not rigorous, so I decided to stay. Why did you go into law?"

"I like to argue, and I'm a sucker for the concept of justice. Before I became a grouch, I was an idealist."

Sara seemed glad for the break and drank a considerable amount of wine during dinner. The subject of her father was not raised until the end, and then by her. "I don't want you to get the wrong idea about my father, Jim. He'd be glad to talk to you, but afterward he'd be inconsolable. He's never gotten over the breakup with my mother."

"That was quite a while ago."

"True, but Dad's a softie. Mom marrying Glen Masters devastated him. He's never gotten over it."

The waitress arrived with dessert menus. "Anyone for dessert?"

They said goodnight outside the restaurant. "Are you going to be okay?" Jim asked.

"Of course. I live close by."

"I meant you seem slightly drunk. It's charming, but I worry you'll walk into a lamppost."

Pat shushed Jim, but Sara reassured him. "It's okay. People tell me that all the time."

"What? Don't walk into lampposts?"

"That they like me better when I've had too much to drink."

"There's a guy in prison name of Dexter Hutchins. He could teach you a thing or two about drink."

"We all have secrets to keep, Jim," Sara said, with a tight wave of her hand. He wondered what she meant by that.

14

He had promised Sara not to try to contact her father, but that didn't preclude googling him. Problem was he didn't know his name. His last name was probably Vincent but that wasn't a certainty, and Jim had no clue of his first name.

He searched for men with the last name of Vincent living in Boston's South End and found eight. Time to call Ernie Farrell.

"Last name may be Vincent. Daughter's name is Sara. Lives in the South End. Teaches piano. See what you can find."

"No problem," Ernie said over the phone.

A few days later. "Sorry, Jim. No luck so far. Are you sure he lives in the South End?"

"I'm not even sure of his last name. Keep trying, please, and let's get together for coffee."

Shuttling back and forth between Mid-Cambridge and Beacon Hill was normally no hardship, nor the walk uphill to Pat's. Today he had a sense of finality as he climbed the hill.

He let himself in, out of breath from the climb. "Pat?"

She emerged from her study. She was holding the manuscript of her memoir. "You'll never guess. The publishing arm of the Bar Association wants to see my book. And I'll get all the credit. Lazy bum."

"I'm jealous. You'll be famous, and I'll be a nobody."

"Your own fault."

"Let's go to the South End to celebrate."

"You're picking the South End for a reason."

"Madam, you have a devious mind."

The walk was longish but pleasant, through the Theatre District and the interlocking streets of the South End until they came to a tiny French bistro they liked. They hadn't reserved but were in luck. The centerpiece of the room was a square counter. Jim and Pat sat in a booth along the walls.

"I wonder if Sara's father lives near here?" he asked once they were seated.

"So that's why you wanted to come here," Pat countered.

"What if he's eating in this restaurant now?"

"Extremely likely," Pat adopted the tone she used when she was indulging him.

"Okay, but if he were, what would he be like?"

"This is your fantasy. You tell me."

"He'd have a build and manner that would blend in with his surroundings so thoroughly that no one would notice him."

"What kind of face?"

"I'm not good on faces. I look for mannerisms. Sara's father would eat hunched over his plate and not raise his head until he finished. Then he would lift his napkin and gently tap his lips, being careful not to attract attention."

Pat pointed with her head. "Like that man across the room."

Jim snuck a glance. "Yes, but he's with a woman. Sara never mentioned that her father has a woman friend."

"Sara hasn't mentioned much of anything about her father."

"True, but I don't think that's him."

"I thought we were playing a game."

"Are you going to have coffee?"

"No."

"Mind if I have another glass of wine?"

"Are you sure?"

"I'm not driving."

They caught a cab home. After a few blocks, Pat said, "This is one of the few times I've seen you drunk. You didn't drink much more than usual, so why are you drunk?"

"Objection. I'm not drunk."

"Are you on the brink of something? Are you on the verge of identifying the killer, is that why?"

"Further away than ever."

Ernie texted the next day that he had narrowed the list of possible Vincents down to two and asked to meet Jim at The Long Gone. Ernie arrived before Jim.

"Four of the men named Vincent are too young to be your man, one is a recent arrival from Seattle, and one is married with three kids. That leaves two possibles. Harry Vincent lives on Appleton Street and has left no discernable digital trail. The other is Charles Vincent on Waltham Street. He was fired from the Boston Public Schools for sexually harassing a student, a charge he denies. He has filed a civil suit against the school system."

The wind had picked up and Jim had broken out his heavier jacket for the first time that year.

"Good work, Ernie. Thanks."

"Are you out of breath? I should have let you get settled."

"That's okay. The air felt good walking here. But I will get coffee. Be right back." Jim went to the counter.

He returned a moment later and stirred a teaspoon of sugar into his espresso. "So it's down to Harry or Charles. Any guesses?"

Ernie shook his head. "To me they are just names."

"Sara has adamantly refused to let me talk to her father, which suggests whoever he is might have something to hide, which would point to Charles."

"His civil suit goes to court on Wednesday. You can go and see for yourself."

"I might do that."

Pat advised against going. "You'll just be disappointed. What can you learn?"

"Probably nothing. But probably nothing is better than definitely nothing, which is what I've got now."

The trial was being held in the Suffolk County Courthouse in downtown Boston. Ernie wanted to see for himself and met Jim there.

They entered the building, passed through the metal detectors, and entered the courtroom where the suit was being heard. Jim had to fight the urge to take the bench.

Charles Vincent appeared to be a man of middle age, slight of build, neither tall nor short. Though it was difficult to tell from the rear.

Jim watched carefully. Vincent trembled, fidgeted, drummed the table with his thumbs. A man on the verge of leaping out of his skin. Once in a while he craned his neck as if searching for someone in the courtroom.

Did his profile resemble Sara's? Could be, same nose, same chin. But the defensive expression, a combination of defiance and despair, was not one Jim had seen on Sara's face.

Jim let his imagination roam. Yes, Charles Vincent could be Sara's father, but it would be a stretch.

When the court recessed for lunch, Jim and Ernie grabbed something to eat at a nearby deli. They sat side-by-side at the counter.

"What do you think?" Jim asked.

"He looked like a pedophile to me. What about you? Think he's Sara's father?"

It was Jim's turn to shrug. "No. But I don't rule him out."

Ernie left after lunch, but Jim briefly stuck around. Courtrooms were like crack to him.

Dinner with Pat in Cambridge. Jim bought a roast chicken at Whole Foods on his way home from the courthouse. There were now three Whole Foods near his townhouse. Whole Foods and Google were taking over the universe.

"Dexter Hutchins goes on trial in two weeks. I don't have much time."

"Jim, I gently remind you that Hutchins may be the killer."

"I'm aware of that, but I still don't think he is."

Jim washed the dishes after dinner. The light coming through the window above the sink was a pale imitation of the light through his window in Vermont. He abruptly turned from the window, frustration on his face and in his voice. "What am I missing? What have I overlooked?"

Jim called Ted Conover the next morning. "I read that you're going ahead with the trial."

"I am. Hutchins has confessed, and there's no evidence to suggest anyone else was involved."

"There's still time."

"Still think it's someone other than Hutchins?"

"A fading hope, but yes. Listen, the pipe that was used to kill Watson, is it possible that Hutchins's fingerprints were not the only ones on it?"

"We checked that out. The pipe came from the construction site behind the Divinity School. The other prints belonged to workers on the site, who all had good alibis. We know what we're doing, Jim."

"Of course you do. Forgive me."

"You're frustrated, I understand. But don't beat yourself up if Hutchins is convicted."

When Jim had been on the bench, he sometimes mentally tried to compensate for an incompetent attorney. He had to stick with the facts as presented when deciding a case, but before then he could try ideas out in his head, see if there were alternate scenarios of the crime that an attorney had overlooked, maybe come up with a question that the attorney had failed to ask. Now Jim tried to compensate for an incompetent amateur detective. That's you, Jim. In his experience, homeless people sometimes bedded down in twos and threes, for safety or warmth. Could Hutchins have an accomplice? Could more than one person have been in on the killing? Maybe Hutchins struck Watson in anger and fled the scene when he realized what he had done, then someone who witnessed the blow finished the job. Unlikely, but possible.

Sara had previously denied seeing or hearing anything out of the ordinary on her walk home the night of the murder. Jim hoped to jog her memory. Buried memories were not uncommon.

They met at The Long Gone, an appropriately named venue when time is running out. She looked at her most serious.

"How are you?" He watched her face.

"Fine. Busy. Why did you want to see me?"

"Dexter Hutchins goes on trial in a week. I'm still not sure he did it, or if he did, that he was alone. I know you've said you didn't see or hear anything out of the ordinary as you walked home that night, but I'm asking you to search your memory for anything you may have forgotten. Any noise, any fleeting glimpse. Think hard."

"You asked me before. Same answer."

"Think again. Try harder."

Something about Sara seemed different. He couldn't place it. The tilt of her head? The attentiveness with which she was watching him? Her expression hadn't changed, still revealed nothing, and then he realized something about her that previously had eluded him. Her imperturbable face masked a vulnerability, a desire to know coupled with a great fear of being hurt. Why hadn't he spotted that before? Surely he knew human nature well enough to know that faces were often masks, surely he knew that. It was the tilt of her head, the lowering of one shoulder, as she sat across from him this morning in The Long Gone that was different, that let him glimpse the vulnerability.

Instinctively he covered her hand with his. Quietly, "Are you okay?"

Her hand trembled. "I want someone to understand."

"Understand what, Sara?"

She spoke so softly he had to lean forward to hear her reply. "I don't trust anyone very much, but I trust you more than most people."

"Why are you telling me this?"

"Because I don't want an innocent man to go to prison."

"Dexter Hutchins?"

Sara turned her head to gaze at the coffee counter, where a barista was pulling levers and shouting names over the sound of hissing steam. She seemed to lose her train of thought. Jim asked again, "Do you mean Dexter Hutchins?"

Sara stared at Jim. The vulnerability he had glimpsed had vanished, replaced by steel and determination. "I want you to meet my father. I'll set something up."

15

Her father was Harry Vincent. He lived in the South End in a redbrick row house on Appleton Street, one of several maze-like streets in a densely packed neighborhood just across the Turnpike from Newbury Street, where Angela Butler, the escapee from The Greater Glory, worked. One could get lost in the South End, and when Jim met Harry Vincent, he saw a man who craved to be lost.

Tall, with the skin-and-bones body of a man who was trying as hard as he could to hide, Harry Vincent was somewhere between the ages of sixty and ninety. He had Sara's face, if Sara were older and defeated.

"Jim, this is my dad."

"How are you, sir?" Jim extended his hand.

Harry Vincent tentatively shook it. He wouldn't meet Jim's eyes. "Fine. Come in, I have some tea."

Harry Vincent's apartment was as crowded as his neighborhood, a tiny room with furniture that had been old-fashioned years ago. A floor lamp by the faded sofa threw a dim, energy-saving light on the room. The one piece of furniture that looked cared for was a standup piano against the wall.

Vincent brought Jim and Sara cups of tea from the kitchen.

"Thank you." Jim took his cup and sat on the sofa next to Sara. "Sara tells me you teach piano."

Vincent took a chair across from Jim and Sara. "Yes, for years and years."

"I was a judge, now I'm a bum."

Vincent didn't crack a smile – maybe Sara's set expression was hereditary, not learned. "I'm a shy man, Judge Randall. I would prefer you get to the point as soon as possible so I can avoid the discomfort of this visit."

Jim was not used to such directness from people he barely knew, and on the bench he had been used to deference.

"As you wish. A man named Dexter Hutchins has been charged with the murder of Melvin Watson. Sara has told me of your summers near Watson's compound and that of Glen Masters, and the unfortunate effects those summers had on your family. I think there may be a connection between then and now."

Vincent considered his answer. "Go on."

"Melvin Watson made a lot of enemies, from what I've learned. There probably are people who are glad he's dead."

"I'm one of them," Vincent interrupted. "I haven't mourned him for a second."

"Which leads to the question, did you kill him?"

"Certainly not. It's hard for me to leave this room, let alone kill someone."

"But I believe the summers you spent near the compounds contain some clue to his murder. Sara has shielded you until now, so I assume you have some light to shed."

"Has Sara told you about Ruth?"

"The child she had as a teenager. Yes, she has." Remembering the pain the subject of Ruth had caused Sara, Jim checked her now. She seemed okay. Apparently it was less painful to hear her father talk about her daughter than to talk about her herself.

"Do you know she put Ruth up for adoption?"

Jim nodded.

"But you don't know who adopted her."

"Correct. I do not."

Vincent came into sharp focus: his face gained definition and his voice became firmer. "When Sara was fifteen, she fell in love with a boy who lived in Melvin Watson's compound. His name was Ben. It was strictly forbidden for members of The Greater Glory to mix with outsiders, but Sara snuck in to be with Ben. Her mother and I disapproved, of course, and when Sara became pregnant, it threatened to tear our family apart. Her mother refused to hear of an abortion or to raise the child in our family, so finally Sara agreed to let Ben's family adopt Ruth. It broke Sara's heart. She never forgave her mother, or me."

Sara corrected him. "Mainly Mom, Dad. She was the one."

"She felt more strongly than I, that's true. I think she was already planning to leave me for Glen Masters and didn't want Sara's child to complicate things."

"This explains a lot," Jim said.

"The rest Sara will have to tell you."

"The rest? What do you mean?"

"That is all I'll tell you."

"Where is Ruth now?"

Harry Vincent shook his head. He wasn't going to say more. Jim looked at Sara.

"Gone," Sara said.

"Gone?"

"No one knows where Ruth is. She escaped from The Greater Glory when she turned fourteen. I don't even know if she's alive."

"How awful for you, Sara. No wonder you didn't want to talk about her."

"You don't know the worst. Ruth ran away because Melvin Watson sexually abused her from the age of eight, and didn't stop until she escaped."

Jim was horrified. "I don't know what to say."

"Ben got word to me of the abuse when I was in grad school. I went to the sheriff, who did absolutely nothing. I told the local weekly, but Watson wielded considerable power in the town, and the editor was terrified of losing advertisers. I told Glen, who by then was married to my mother, but he claimed to be powerless, and Mom refused to talk about it. I tried to take Ruth away, but Watson kept all his girls hidden and denied everything. I felt helpless. I lived with that feeling for years."

"Where is Ben now?"

"No one knows. He left The Greater Glory years ago. I received one letter from him postmarked Denmark. He told me he was heading to India. I never heard from him again."

"My heart goes out to you, Sara, and to you, sir. This must have been hard on you, too."

Vincent nodded. "I hated to see Sara suffer. I hated to see what this did to her. She used to radiate curiosity about people and the world around her, then she closed down. It broke my heart."

It was as if the air had been sucked out of the room, leaving nothing for sound waves to travel in. Jim had never heard such silence.

Harry Vincent stood and collected Jim's cup; he had not touched his tea. "I don't mean to be rude, but my capacity for having company in my home has been exceeded. Please leave."

"Of course." Jim stood. "Thank you for helping me. I am very grateful. Are you coming, Sara?"

"No, I'm staying. Dad and I have some catching up to do."

Jim didn't have it in him to call and tell Pat he was on the way. How awful for Sara. How awful for her father. And most of all how awful for Ruth. Sickening. Horrifying.

Pat heard him unlocking the door and came to open it. She took one look at his face and ushered him into the living room. "Don't say anything. Sit and I'll get you a glass of wine."

He sat in her most comfortable chair.

She emerged from the kitchen. "It was awful?" She handed him the wine.

"Awful. The father of Sara's daughter, Ruth, was a boy from Watson's compound. The boy's family adopted her, and when Ruth was eight, Watson started abusing her. Sara doesn't know where she is, doesn't even know if she's alive. She ran away years ago."

"How horrible. I can't imagine."

"Me either. You think you've heard it all. All I can do is shake my head."

"We'll go out to dinner, have a nice evening together."

He stood and hugged her. "Pat," was all he could manage to say.

They ate at the narrow bistro at the base of the hill. Somewhere familiar. Pat waited to speak until they were well into their meal. What she said was, "Considering what you learned today, Sara has to be a suspect. She certainly had motive."

"To kill Watson? I'm not ready to make that leap."

"Why, Jim? By taking you to meet her father, she more or less confessed."

"That's not true."

"Think, Jim. I know you like her, but think carefully. She knew that if you heard what her father had to say, you'd realize she had reason to want Watson dead. Why do you think she refused to let you meet her father for so long?"

"I don't want to believe that about Sara."

"Let's not discuss it now. I promised you a nice evening."

Jim wanly smiled. "It's okay, Pat. I'm fine."

She said nothing more until they were undressing for bed. "One more thing. Why did Sara wait until now to introduce you to her father?"

"She said she didn't want an innocent man to go to prison."

"Exactly. Her conscience overcame her instinct for self-preservation. If she didn't have anything to hide, you would have met her father long ago. She handed you her confession today."

"I hate to think that."

"You're doing something you never did on the bench. You're letting your heart rule your head."

"Sara has suffered a lot."

"And one can empathize with her, but she's now the prime suspect."

Since Jim had taken off his judicial robe and put down his gavel, his emotional defenses were far weaker than before. Was Pat right? Was he letting his heart rule his head? Sara had suffered greatly, that was for sure, but did that mean she was innocent? Should he report her to Ted? Turn Sara in? Did he know enough? Did he have the right?

He had to give her a chance to explain. No trusting his gut this time, no flying by the seat of his pants. If Pat was right, then his instincts about Sara had been wrong.

Sara refused to see him, wouldn't take his phone calls, answer his texts. He could ambush her, stop by her office, sneak into a lecture. He had done both before; why did the thought of doing so now repel him? Was it out of concern for her well-being, or was he afraid of what he would learn?

He didn't like himself when he dithered, he liked himself better when he was decisive, as he had been on the bench. As he was whenever he solved a case involving someone he hated, so easy to be decisive when you hate.

Pat didn't ask him about Sara again. She let Jim decide what to do in his own way. The solution came to him at The Long Gone. Of course, The Long Gone; where else? He texted her.

> I hate to do this but I will go to the DA with what I now know unless you tell me everything. Nothing held back. I won't like it but I'll do it.

The reply came at once, as if she had been waiting for him. "Meet me behind the Divinity School at 7." Followed moments later by a single word, "Asshole."

16

The construction work behind the Divinity School was ongoing, which meant the scene did not look the same as it had the night of the murder. Ditches, including the ditch where Watson's body had been discovered, had been filled in. But the overall scene remained the same. A scattering of equipment sheds, gashes in the earth that had yet to be filled, a pre-existing greenhouse, and the beginnings of a landscaped vest-pocket park. The symbolism was stark: dirt behind the divine, the underbelly of the gods, and science buildings and research labs beyond the construction site. Gods, underbelly, science, in a row.

The light at that time of evening at that time of year was haunting, tentative, an in-between light. A make-up-your-mind light. A spill-the-beans light. Jim arrived at the site before Sara.

She approached from the east, out of the shadows. By a trick of light she seemed transparent one moment, opaque the next. Then Jim could see her face, and he was shocked to see she no longer wore a mask. She looked ineffably sad, but maybe that, too, was a trick of light.

She stopped in front of Jim.

"Hello, Jim."

"Thanks for meeting me."

"You left me little choice."

"Sara, I like you in case you can't tell and I don't like doing this to you, but you knew what introducing me to your father would lead to, which is why you hesitated for so long, am I correct?"

"Of course you are. I wasn't fooling anybody, least of all Pat or you. I was going to tell you the whole story when we met with Dad, but I chickened out. Are you ready?"

"Go."

"Over here." She walked deeper into the construction site and stopped behind an equipment shed. In the shadows, Sara's gesture was hard to see. "It was here, behind this shed, that I found Melvin Watson."

"Start at the beginning."

He could hear but not see Sara take a deep breath.

"The night of the panel, after we had a drink in the Square, I was walking home past the Divinty School when I heard a man scream. I stopped and listened, unsure of what I had heard. This time I heard groaning. I hurried towards the sound and saw a shabbily dressed man running away and a man lying in a ditch, groaning. I came closer and saw that the man was Melvin Watson. He groaned again. I leaned close to him. 'Can you hear me? It's Sara Vincent. Who did this to you?' It was dark, but I could see blood on his head, his face. 'Help me,' he moaned."

"I will, but first tell me where Ruth is."

"Ruth?"

"'My daughter. Where is she?'"

"I don't know, I swear. Help me."

"I felt possessed. I shook him by the shoulders and screamed, 'Tell me!'"

"I don't know. Please, Sara."

"Rage consumed me. He might be telling the truth, he might not know where she was, but he had molested her, he had driven her away. All the hatred I had bottled up erupted, and I could picture myself hitting him again and again until I crushed his skull. What happened next was like watching a slow-motion movie of myself. I saw myself searching for something to crush his skull with, I saw myself picking up a piece of pipe that was lying in the ditch, and I saw myself hit him over and over in the head until he stopped groaning. Only then did I realize what I had done."

She stopped. He wished he could clearly see her face.

"Dexter Hutchins's fingerprints were on the pipe. Why weren't yours?"

"I took the pipe home with me and disposed of it in the trash. He must have used a different piece of pipe. It was a construction site."

"Disposing of the pipe shows presence of mind, bringing it closer to first-degree murder instead of second. But it's borderline, and your attorney can argue that you were in the throes of uncontrollable anger when you hit him and only came to your senses afterwards. Tell me, did you invite Watson to be on the panel with the intent to kill him?"

"No. I planned to get him alone and confront him. I had a whole litany of sins stored up to unload on his sorry head, instead I beat his head with a pipe until he was dead. And you know what? I'm not at all sorry. I'm sorry I lied, to you and others, but I'm not sorry he's dead."

Jim waited to see if there was more. She seemed relieved to have confessed.

There was no need to hurry.

"That's all, Jim. Now you know everything."

"When you're ready, I'll call the DA."

"I'm ready. Go ahead."

Jim dialed Ted. No answer. Just before Jim hung up, Ted answered, out of breath. "I just walked in the door. What's up?"

"Sara Vincent is standing here with me. We're behind the Divinity School. Sara has just confessed to murdering Melvin Watson."

*

Sara spent the night in jail and was arraigned the following day. She pleaded not guilty to give herself bargaining leverage. Bail was set at $500,000. She couldn't make bail.

"Why do I feel so awful?" Jim asked Pat that night in Cambridge.

"Because you liked Sara. Because you believed in her."

"I still think she is fundamentally a good person. She's an example of how extreme provocation can make a good person do dreadful things."

"What's going to happen to Dexter Hutchins?"

"Ted will reduce the charges to assault and battery. He'll serve the bulk of his time in a mental hospital. If he stays clean, Ted will recommend probation for the remainder of his sentence."

"And Sara?"

"Ted will be fair. He's a good man, not someone who's looking to put notches on his belt. I wouldn't be surprised to see a plea bargain that takes the mitigating circumstances into account."

"A philosophy professor who murders a predatory preacher. Not something you see everyday," Pat said.

"Sara was a victim too, remember. The feud between Watson and Masters split her family apart and shielded Watson while he molested her daughter. Sara had plenty of reason to want Watson dead, but she didn't kill him until Dexter Hutchins put him in a ditch."

"She may not be as innocent as you make her sound. She did invite Watson to be on the panel. How do you know her plan wasn't to kill him after the panel?"

"Why did she have a drink with us in the Square if that was her plan?"

"I don't know. All I know is that Ted may not want to plea bargain until he learns all the facts."

"I agree."

"What's next?"

"I'm going up to Maine to tell the Masterses."

17

Jim drove north alone on a dull gray morning. Nothing against Maine, but he didn't plan to rush back. When he arrived at The Greater Good three hours later, he was surprised to see a sturdy gate blocking the entrance. That hadn't been there before, had it? He remembered a rope, a sign, not a gate. Or was he thinking of the border between the two Greaters?

Not only a gate, but an intercom. He buzzed. "Yes?" A woman's voice.

"I'm here to see Glen Masters. My name is Jim Randall."

The gate unlatched, and Jim drove through. Once inside, The Greater Good looked the same as before: no people in sight, and modest cabins in a circle. Jim parked at Masters's house and knocked on the front door.

Rachel Masters opened it. "Glen's not home."

"May I come in?"

"He won't be back for a couple of hours."

"Then I'll wait in the car. I need to talk to both of you."

Rachel stood aside. "You'd better come in."

She seemed diminished in the living room without Glen, a supporting actor when the lead actor is offstage. "I have work to do, but would you like some coffee?"

"Please. And can I use your bathroom?"

She showed him where it was, off the short hall leading to the bedrooms. The bathroom had the cluttered feel of a college dorm room, towels on the floor, soap in the sink. As he rinsed his hands, he saw an angry man in the mirror. He needed to control himself, he had not come to lecture or chastize the Masterses but to inform them. Yet he could not pretend he didn't want to tell them what shitty parents they had been. Rachel, a shitty parent because she was willing to sacrifice her will, her daughter, and her granddaughter to get certainty in her life; Glen because...and here, Jim was admittedly guessing although he was pretty sure he was right...maximizing his power was more important to him than people.

He stepped out of the bathroom. He could hear Rachel in the kitchen, and he took the opportunity to peek in the master bedroom (aptly named for once). What struck him was how devoid of religious symbols it was: no cross above the bed, no pictures of baby Jesus, not even a bible in sight. The bed was rumpled, the window shades drawn. A cheap motel room before the maid cleans it.

Jim returned to the living room.

"Coffee's on the table," Rachel said when she saw Jim.

"Thanks."

"You have something about Sara to tell us?"

"I'd prefer to wait and tell you both at once."

"Is she dead?"

"No, she's alive."

Jim sat at the table in the living room. Glen's laptop was open; the screensaver was Jesus. Rachel joined Jim at the table.

Her face was thoughtful, troubled. "Sara told you about Ruth, didn't she?"

"Yes."

"You must think badly of me and Glen."

"Again, let's wait until he gets here."

"I have many regrets," she said.

"Don't we all?"

"Some more than others."

"I want you to understand. Glen could not, would not, allow a child conceived by his fifteen-year-old stepdaughter to live in his house. His moral authority with his followers would be ruined. Please understand."

"I understand his attitude. What I can't understand is yours."

"I love Glen. I had shattered my marriage for him. How could I turn my back on him?"

"For the sake of your daughter?"

"Her baby was conceived in sin, Judge Randall. I love Sara, but what she did was wrong."

"I may not see it that way, but I didn't come to lecture you. You have suffered, too, not just Sara."

"But she is okay, isn't she?"

"She's neither sick nor dead."

Rachel turned her head. All the color had drained from her face. A sad, sad woman. The Greater Good, my ass.

The front door opened and Glen Masters stomped in. "Whose car is that out front?" he stormed. He stopped when he saw Jim at the table. "What are you doing here? I told you never to come back."

Rachel, for the first time in Jim's hearing, spoke with quiet authority. "The Judge has something to tell us. Something to do with Sara."

Glen glared at Jim. "Is that right?"

"Sit down. This won't be easy for either of you."

Glen sat, but he didn't look happy. "We have a nice life here if you'd leave us alone."

"Before I tell you about Sara, let me clarify one thing. Have you merged The Greater Glory with The Greater Good?"

"Why is that your business?"

"It would explain a lot. It would reinforce my opinion."

"Of what?"

"You. Your motives."

"I didn't kill Watson, if that's what you're thinking."

"No, Sara did."

Glen looked puzzled, Rachel stricken.

"I'm sorry to be the one to tell you."

Glen regained his voice. "Sara couldn't kill anybody. That's ridiculous."

"She confessed and turned herself in to the DA."

"No!" Rachel cried.

"I'm afraid so. Are you ready for me to explain or shall I wait a moment?"

Glen stole a quick look at Rachel. "Go ahead."

"Mrs. Masters?" Jim asked. She nodded.

Jim took them through it step by step. The panel at the Divinity School, Sara walking home and hearing a man scream, finding Watson bleeding in a ditch, and hitting him repeatedly over the head until he was dead. The Masterses listened somberly.

When Jim had finished, Rachel cried silently. Glen looked diminished, not at all in charge.

"What will happen to her?" Glen asked.

"That remains to be seen. The charge is second-degree murder, which presumes intent to kill with no premeditation.

Under the circumstances, my guess is she will be sentenced to twenty-five years to life, with the possibility of parole after fifteen. It's up to the judge."

"We can't afford an attorney," Glen said.

"She can, and I've put her in touch with a good one."

Rachel had trouble speaking. "This is my fault. I allowed this to happen."

Glen Masters tried to comfort her. "Don't blame yourself. Sara is a grown woman. She made her own choices."

Rachel turned on him. "If you hadn't driven her away, if you hadn't made me choose between her or you."

"Rachel?" Glen looked bewildered.

"I mean it, Glen. We failed her."

Jim stood from the table. "I'll leave you two alone. Is there anything you want me to tell Sara?"

"Tell her I love her. She won't believe me, but I do," Rachel said.

Glen shook his head, "I have nothing to say to her. She made her own bed, now she has to lie in it."

Jim walked to the front door. "If you want to contact her, she's in the Middlesex County Jail, awaiting trial. Good luck to both of you."

Rachel had the look of a doomed woman. Glen had the look of a man aggrieved. The world was against him, including his stepdaughter.

Goodbye and good riddance, Jim thought as he climbed in his car. He felt sorry for Rachel. She had forfeited her duties as a mother but not her capacity for suffering as a mother. He did not feel sorry for Glen.

*

Prison hardens many people; it softened Sara. Her face had expression, one of the expressions was worry, but another was relief. "Why did you want to see me?" she asked Jim in the visitors room.

"I went to see your mother and stepfather and told them what had happened. Your mother was devastated by the news. She blames herself. Your stepfather was less kind."

"Will my mother come to see me?"

"I don't know. Do you want her to?"

"I'm not sure. Probably not, probably it would do no good."

"Anyway, she said to tell you she loves you."

Sara pinched her lips. "I guess that's good."

"She's a weak woman, Sara, but she did the best she could."

"I don't judge her, but I'm not going to pretend that loving me makes her a good mother. Glen's hold on her was stronger than her love for me. But it's nice to hear her say that."

"Are you doing okay?"

"It's a new experience. My teaching days are over, but I'm still a professor at heart and being in jail is instructional from a philosophical point of view."

Jim smiled. "That's what I like about you, Sara."

"I don't know why you would. I've realized since I've been in here that I don't have much personality. I'm working on it."

"Personality is overrated. Has the attorney I recommended come to see you?"

"Yes. He seems fine."

"I went to law school with him. He's one of the best."

"I'm not going to fight this, Jim."

"I know. But Thad will make sure the court considers the mitigating circumstances."

"Will you come to visit me, Jim?"

"Of course."

"Bring Kant."

"Screw Kant. I'll bring Cicero."

Their time was up. As Jim stood to leave, Sara said, "How is Pat? I really admire her."

"Me too. She's doing fine. Feels badly for you."

Outside the courthouse, he stood on the sidewalk and considered which way to go: Beacon Hill or home. What decided him on Pat's was the premonition that walking past the live poultry shop and Beauty Shop Row on this day would be depressing rather than therapeutic, and he wanted to save them for when he needed solace in the future.

Made in the USA
Middletown, DE
16 December 2020

28052840R00113